THE STONEBRIDGE MYSTERIES

-6-

ALL AT SEA

CHRIS MCDONALD

RED DOG
UK

Published by RED DOG PRESS 2022

First Edition

Hardback ISBN 978-1-914480-91-1
Paperback ISBN 978-1-914480-89-8
Ebook ISBN 978-1-914480-90-4

www.reddogpress.co.uk

MORE IN THE SERIES

The Curious Dispatch of Daniel Costello

Dead in the Water

Meat is Murder

The Case of the Missing Firefly

Mistletoe and Crime

1

DISASTER

ADAM HATED PACKING. Always had done. Always would do. Of course, he was looking forward to what came after—the cruise. Eight nights on the open water, stopping at various European cities before docking in Venice. A short train journey later, he'd be on the banks of Lake Garda, marrying the love of his life.

His mother had been slightly disappointed by the fact that they'd decided on a destination wedding, but neither Adam nor Helena wanted a big fuss. They'd rather spend their money on a small ceremony with a stunning backdrop than fill a tent with second cousins and great aunts who they hadn't spoken to in ten years, and probably would never see again.

No. Tying the knot in front of people they actually cared about was far preferable, and doing it with the Italian sun on their faces even more so.

They'd flown out a couple of times, to assess the location, sort out the paperwork, and meet the vicar who would be performing the ceremony. Each time, Adam's heart had soared at the view from the medieval castle on the shore of Malcesine; the endless stretch of water, the snow-capped mountains that seemed to scratch the sky, the pretty Mediterranean houses with those terracotta rooftops he loved so much.

It was all so perfect.

The plan had been to fly there a few days before the ceremony to give them time to sort the last-minute things out, but then Adam's mum had surprised them with a once in a lifetime opportunity.

Two first class tickets aboard The Elysian.

1

Adam had scolded her at first, castigating her for spending what he presumed was an unholy amount of money, especially since she'd already chipped in for the wedding. But, no argument with a woman of a certain age about money gets won, especially if that woman is Northern Irish—the sweetest old lady in the land can turn into Deborah Meaden at the mention of cash.

And so, Adam found himself packing for the trip. As well as what he needed for the wedding (suit, tie, smart shoes), he was now also having to think about the journey by boat.

Would it be cold while they were journeying, or hot? Would he need a woolly hat or shorts? These were questions he couldn't answer, so he found himself randomly opening drawers, gazing in with little enthusiasm before closing them again.

Helena would know.

She was like The Flash with this stuff. Set her off, and before you knew it, your case was packed, zipped and labelled.

Adam threw down a pair of goggles he'd somehow acquired, despite not having swum for the best part of a decade (probably in one of Mr McCall's horrific PE lessons at school—even now, the thought of the cold, chlorinated water made him shiver). He made his way to the living room to ask for Helena's advice.

Except, Helena was in no condition to give advice.

She was lying on the sofa, cheeks stained black by running mascara. She looked like one of the band members from My Chemical Romance, though of course he didn't mention that particular thought. Instead, he rushed to her side.

'What's wrong?' he asked, taking hold of her hand.

'That was the dress shop,' she mumbled between sobs. 'The lady who does the alterations called in sick today, and won't be back until the start of the week. They can't get anyone else which means my dress won't be ready before the cruise.'

'They know your measurements, though. Mum can grab it and bring it with her on the plane.' Even as he said it, Adam knew he was underestimating the enormity of this particular disaster.

Helena shook her head.

'The thought of the dress not fitting on the day is awful. I'd be thinking about it the whole time we were on the boat. I need to go to the fitting.'

Adam nodded. He'd heard horror stories of how usually reasonable women became monsters during the run up to their wedding. Thankfully, Helena had remained her cool, normal self, and so he knew how much the dress meant to her if she was reacting like this.

'It's cool. I'll phone the company and see if we can rearrange the cruise.'

He was pulled into a tight hug and felt Helena's lips on his cheek. He returned to the bedroom to find his phone, and pulled up the email confirmation. Finding the customer services number, he dialled.

The company had chosen a lullaby version of a Foo Fighters song for their hold music, causing Adam to feel simultaneously impressed at their taste in music, and sleepy.

After a short wait, the music was replaced by a slightly accented voice—Nordic, he thought. Adam relayed his plight, and though the voice on the other side of the phone was sympathetic, they were also firm on their stance.

Because the planned journey was only a few days away, there was nothing that could be done.

Adam thanked the man on the other end of the phone and hung up, before delivering the news to Helena, who reacted by crying again.

'I'm so sorry,' she managed between sobs. 'You must think I'm a nightmare.'

'Not at all,' he placated her, stroking the back of her hand softly.

After a few minutes, she calmed enough to suggest an alternative.

'Do you think Colin would go with you?'

'I'm sure Colin wouldn't say no to a free cruise,' Adam laughed. 'The big man loves the sea.'

'You should call him,' she said. 'If he can't go, then I'll just have to trust the dress will be okay. I don't want to waste your mum's money.'

Adam once again reached for his phone, this time dialling the number of his best friend and one-time partner in crime (solving).

Over the past couple of years, they'd taken on the somewhat unlikely role of unofficial Stonebridge detectives, when people had come to them with problems that the police had written off as unworthy of their time.

Adam and Colin had solved five cases in their career to date, but hadn't been called upon in nearly six months, not since last Christmas. Adam was partly thankful, as he'd had a lot on his plate, what with the wedding and running his own business. Still, there was something exhilarating about the tangled web of a case that he missed.

He and Colin had a short conversation, that ended with his friend agreeing to come on the cruise, as long as Adam was willing to accept some money in return. He also offered to change the name on his flight to Helena's so that she could fly to Italy with Colin's girlfriend, Anna, who would make sure she got to the alter on time.

'Everything has worked out,' Adam said to Helena, setting the phone on the table and relaying the content of their conversation.

'Just promise me you won't get into any trouble,' she replied.

Adam laughed, and promised her that he certainly wouldn't be looking for any.

The unfortunate truth, however, was that trouble often found Adam, whether he went looking for it or not.

2

BON VOYAGE

THE ELYSIAN WAS breath-taking. Though the ship was a few years old, it looked like it had sailed here straight from the shipyard it had just been built in. The town's harbour was usually reserved for small fishing vessels and the occasional jet skier, so the sight of this huge ocean liner was almost laughable. It was like something from another planet. The vast body was painted glacier white, and gleamed in the Stonebridge sunshine. The various decks rose high into the sky, and Colin could hear jolly music and laughter as he waited to board with Adam. Spirits were high, even with the keen-eyed seagulls squawking above their heads, hoping that such a large gathering of people might yield a decent return in the dropped food department.

Once boarding began, the operation was sleek and well-oiled, and before they knew it, their cases had been whisked away at the check-in desk, and they were quickly led away by a friendly, uniformed worker with a Claudia Winkleman fringe.

The interior of the ship was breathtaking, opulence dripping from every square millimetre. The place was polished to within an inch of its life; the white marble underfoot dazzling. Huge spiral staircases led to higher floors, each step emitting a soft white glow, the central column made up of thousands of twinkling LEDs. A smattering of chandeliers filled the space with light, the biggest and most lavish taking up most of the centre of the ceiling, itself painted in an imitation of Michelangelo's most famous work—The Creation of Adam.

They could have stood for a couple more hours and not managed to take in every detail of the decadence. Adam nodded at faux-Claudia and she ushered them across the cavernous space towards a bank of lifts.

They entered the lift, which was purposefully decorated in an art deco style; wooden panelled, complete with a shuttered door and one of those circular handles instead of buttons. It made Adam think of the Titanic, which was not a comforting notion at all. Claudia worked the handle, and the lift started to ascend, taking them noiselessly to the top deck. From here, they could see every detail of their town and beyond.

They leaned against the barrier, waved a dramatic goodbye and pretended to cry, hugging each other as if leaving for war, as Claudia looked on, not knowing what to do.

'Gentlemen, if you'll follow me,' she said, eventually, with a slight tremor in her voice.

Colin and Adam followed her to the stern of the ship, and stopped behind her when she pulled a key card from her pocket. She tapped it on the sensor beside a cabin door, which slid open.

'Your quarters for the next eight nights,' she said, handing the key to Adam, before bowing (bowing!) and backing away from them.

'Quarters' was underselling it, by some distance.

The Bridal Suite of The Elysian could've been lifted straight from one of the world's six-star hotels. The door opened into an enormous living space. The walls were painted a tasteful cream, letting the furniture do the talking. A purple, velvet sofa and accompanying armchair presided over a marble table, upon which sat a few classic novels, artfully arranged as if for a photoshoot. The room opened up into a well-appointed kitchen which looked a bit more modern, but still classy. The room was stunning, yet it didn't compare to the bedroom.

The king-sized bed was placed so that, upon waking, one could survey the endless ocean through a wall of glass. A little balcony could be accessed by another door, upon which sat a small table and a couple of chairs. The en-suite bathroom was the size of Adam's kitchen at home, and when he stood inspecting his kingdom, a little pang of sadness snagged at his chest at the thought of his wife-to-be missing out on such an adventure.

'I'm happy with the sofa,' Colin said, poking his head into the bedroom.

'I'm happy with you on the sofa, too,' Adam laughed. 'I don't want those cheesy feet stinking out a room this good!'

'Shut up,' Colin laughed, flinging a plump pillow in Adam's direction. 'Did you know you were going to be living in this much luxury?'

'No. Mum undersold it. Probably knew I'd make her take it back if I had've done!'

'Well, selfishly, I'm pleased she kept it hidden.'

They left the bedroom and sat down in the living space. On the table, beside the books, was a bottle of champagne in a frosted bucket, and two flutes. Adam had always feared popping a cork, as he thought it might result in losing an eye, so left Colin in charge. Ever reliable, he managed to release the cork with minimal effort, and without spilling a single drop.

Glasses full, they toasted their trip.

'Here's to you and Helena,' Colin said, raising a glass.

'And staying out of trouble,' Adam added.

After a few sips, they noted an invite on the table. Apparently, there was to be a tasting menu for first class passengers laid on in the Augustine Lounge that evening.

'A tasting menu?' Adam sighed. 'It's going to be all fancy crap and tiny portions, isn't it?'

ENTERING THE AUGUSTINE Lounge felt like walking into a room at Buckingham Palace, or so Adam imagined. He felt like a pleb from the get go.

In his mind, the cruise was going to be a relaxing time, filled with endless days on a sun lounger, punctuated only by trips to the bar or the on-board cinema. And, so he had packed accordingly. His suitcase had been filled with T-shirts, shorts and not much else. On the off chance he'd fancied getting dressed up (and mostly at Helena's insistence), he'd thrown in a pair of jeans and a flannel shirt, both of which he was wearing now. Everyone else was either wearing an expensive-looking suit or a fancy evening gown. Some of the women even had fascinators perched on their heads, like they were heading to a day at the races.

The only saving grace was that Colin was also sporting a casual look. They looked like a pair of party crashers, and Adam was sure they were going to be asked for identification sooner rather than later.

A man in a full tuxedo sat behind a grand piano, tickling the ivories, while the first-class passengers sipped from wine glasses and got to know each other. Adam accepted his own glass from a passing waiter, and passed one to Colin.

'Maybe if we get drunk quickly, this will be less awkward,' Adam suggested, before raising the glass to his lips, downing the contents and fighting to keep an enormous burp at bay.

'That's one way to do it,' Colin said, before following suit and grabbing two more glasses from a different waiter.

From the front of the grand room, the ting of silverware striking the stem of a glass sounded, and the chatter died away. All eyes turned to the man responsible.

'Hello, everyone,' said the man. 'My name is Edd Graham-Hyde, and I am the captain of the ship. I want to wish you all a pleasant journey on board The Elysian, and want you to know that no request shall go unanswered. If we can do something to make your stay with us unforgettable, we will. We'll go overboard for you, though, not literally.'

This joke, that Adam assumed he said during every introduction, produced a hearty laugh from around the room. The man was tall and spoke with a hint of a German accent, and seemed to have finished his short toast, as he gave a small salute before leaving the front of the room and beginning to mingle.

A short while later, the assembled guests were asked to take a seat at one of the circular tables. Each table seated eight, and Adam and Colin simply picked the one they were closest to. The rest of the seats filled, and Adam suppressed a sigh.

Of course, he'd been saddled with the crazy lady.

He'd noticed her while boarding earlier in the day. Her mane of white hair and kooky pastel glasses were more than enough to make her stand out, but even stranger was the fact she had been carrying a framed painting. The same framed painting which stood on a portable easel beside Adam now.

As they waited for the first course to arrive, they took it in turns to introduce themselves, though one in particular needed no such introduction.

Vaughn McClusky was in many movies Adam loved—mostly action, though he'd shown he could turn in a good comedic performance, too. He seemed to be constantly on the cusp of a huge starring role that, sadly, had never come. Adam had often presumed that actors looked good thanks to make up and a range of tonics, but up close, he could see that Vaughn's good looks were thanks to an angular jaw and striking green eyes.

The man next to him was small and wiry, probably in his fifties, and was positively buzzing with nervous energy. A bushy moustache obscured most of his mouth, and when he spoke, his words poured forth in an American drawl. He introduced himself as Tex Rivera. Adam supposed it was a false name.

Henry Carver-Clark was next. His suit looked like the most expensive in the room, and when he spoke, he sounded like Prince Charles, despite being in his early 20s. He was tall and bony and, from the sounds of it, had never been told 'no' as a child. He made some quip about how the piano player was sticking to the tried and tested same-old, same-old, and only got a few grunts in reply. Adam didn't much like him.

He *did,* however, very much like the next two.

Isiah Lookman wore his suit casually. No tie, top button open. Adam would bet no socks, too, which he wasn't usually a fan of, but got the feeling that this guy could pull it off. His hair was shaved tight to his scalp, except for a strip up the middle which was dyed a bright red. Isiah cracked a little joke at his own expense, and the table laughed. He had an easy air about him.

And if Isiah was easy to like, Sean O'Connell was doubly so. He spoke with a thick Southern Irish accent and looked somewhat out of his element. The suit he wore looked cheap and shabby; shiny around the elbows and stained on the lapels. He sat at an angle, with one arm draped over the back of the chair. He occasionally tucked a stray strand of his curly ginger hair behind an ear, and looked like he was already a few Guinness's deep.

Adam and Colin were the last to introduce themselves, and finished just in time. The first courses were arriving.

Adam winced at what was set in front of him.

'Cèpe mushroom with Jerusalem artichoke and truffle,' the waiter said with a bow. Seconds later, the sommelier made an appearance and filled their glasses with a perfectly paired red wine, while giving them information about the type of grape used and the process of manufacture of this particular variety.

All Adam wanted was a can of coke and a cheeseburger. It was going to be a long night.

As the scant offerings were devoured by the rest of the table and picked at by Adam, Tex brought up the painting.

'What's with the print of Grachten?' he said.

'Grachten? Isn't that one of the chicks from Mean Girls?' Isiah quipped.

'That's Gretchen Wieners, you ignoramus,' Sean said, causing the table to howl with laughter.

'You know it?' Maggie asked Tex, in reply to his original question.

'I'm an art dealer, of course I know it! It was Otto Van Schaik's masterpiece, though of course it was sold shortly after the time of painting, having spent only a matter of months in a gallery.'

'Seems like you know your stuff,' the old lady smiled. 'Why not take a closer look?'

Tex got up and moved around the table. He peered closely at the details of the painting, from the signature in the bottom right-hand corner to the turquoise-coloured canals depicted in thick brushstrokes.

'You're kidding me,' he muttered, before turning to Maggie. 'You *own* it?!'

'It's been in my family for generations.'

'And you just, what, carry it about with you?'

'Yes. It makes me smile every time I look at it. What's the point of keeping it in storage, or at home? It's an excellent conversation starter, too.'

'It is magnificent,' Tex agreed. 'But, do you know how much it's worth?'

'Something like four million,' she said, breezily. 'At least, that's what the last valuation said.'

The table erupted in a quiet furore at the casualness with which the figure was said, like it was no more than loose change, and Adam wondered if she'd made a mistake in disclosing the princely sum.

The rest of the night passed quickly. Wine flowed and so did conversation, and before long, Adam found himself tipsily stumbling into the huge bed. Out of the windows, he watched the stars twinkle and swirl, before closing his eyes and letting sleep claim him.

3

THE INEVITABLE BOTHER

COLIN AWOKE WITH a start. The room was dark and when he checked his watch, he saw that it was shortly after three in the morning. His head swam a little from the sheer amount of wine consumed a couple of hours previously, his mouth was dry and he couldn't figure what had woken him up.

He wracked his brain, and remembered a dream that ended in a scream. Had the scream been real? Was Adam in trouble?

Quickly, he pushed himself off the luxurious sofa, staggered across to the bedroom and turned the handle. He snuck in to find Adam on his side, snoring loudly with one arm hanging down the side of the bed, dead to the world.

Colin pulled the door closed again and looked around. Maybe it *had* been his dream that had woken him, but a feeling was tugging at his chest, telling him that something was wrong.

He checked the rest of the suite, before opening the door and heading outside onto the deck. He leaned against the barrier for a while and took a moment to appreciate the star-filled sky, the lack of land and the sheer vastness of the sea. The cool wind felt nice against his clammy skin, and he basked in it for a few more minutes, before turning back to his room.

Except, as he turned, something caught his eye.

The door to the next cabin along was open, which struck him as odd at this time of night. He walked over to it, and gasped at what he saw.

Lying on the thick carpeted floor of the suite was Maggie.

Her arms were above her head, like she'd been frozen in the middle of a Mexican Wave, and her monogramed silk pyjamas had ridden up, revealing a little tattoo to the left of her bellybutton. Her face was frozen in a rictus of pain, and Colin fell to his knees beside her and checked for a pulse.

Luckily, the faint throb of flowing blood was present at her wrist, and after thirty seconds, Colin let her hand fall gently to the floor. He wracked his brain for what to do next.

He didn't want to move her in case she had suffered spinal injuries, and knew the best thing to do was leave her where she was. The wind blowing in off the ocean was cold though, so he went to her bedroom and pulled the heavy duvet off, placing it over her where she lay.

As he was about to go and get Adam, the old lady began muttering groggily. She opened one eye slowly, and then the other, and cried out in fear when she saw Colin.

'It's okay,' he said, soothingly, holding up his hands like an arrested man. 'You've had a fall. It's Colin, we met at the dinner earlier. Do you remember? I'm trying to help you.'

'No… no…' She tried to push herself up and away from him.

'Try to stay relaxed,' he whispered. 'In a minute, I'm going to go and find someone who can check you over.'

He kneeled down beside her and stroked her hair, as one would a small child who was distressed. She closed her eyes again.

'Do you remember what happened?' Colin asked. 'Were you on your way out for a little midnight stroll?'

'A knock,' she muttered. 'A knock.'

'Someone knocked on your door?'

'Mmhmm.'

'And you answered it?'

'Yes.'

'Who was it?' Colin asked.

'Didn't see them. Too dark. Dressed in black. They shoved me and I think I banged my head. Next thing, you've woken me up.'

'Did they say anything?'

'No. As soon as I opened it, they pushed me over. That's all I can remember.'

Colin could see the old lady didn't know what happened next, and didn't want to cause any more distress by pushing her further. As he tried to keep her calm, he wondered why anyone would ram an old lady over in the middle of the night.

And then it hit him.

It was obvious.

The painting.

He pushed himself up from the floor and walked further into the room. The easel was standing near her bed, but the framed painting was nowhere to be seen.

He went to the kitchen and poured water into a glass, and took it to Maggie.

'It's gone, isn't it?' she said, when she'd taken a sip.

'Yes,' Colin nodded.

Her eyes immediately began to well and she started to sob, tear tracks travelling down her wrinkled skin. Colin rubbed her shoulder, and in a moment of being unsure how best to comfort her, said: 'The police will find it.'

She shook her head. 'I was told about that before I came on the boat. My son warned me. Told me I was being stupid taking it with me, that because it's international waters, there won't be much the police can do.'

'But, it's a boat. It's not like whoever took it can have got very far. Surely the captain can just search everyone's rooms.'

She stayed quiet, so Colin spoke again.

'Look, Adam and I have solved a few crimes back home. We'll find the painting for you.'

'No,' she said, 'I wouldn't want to put you through any bother. Besides, where would you even start?' she asked.

Colin was thinking about their dinner table. It was clear that Maggie wasn't in possession of the painting, and neither were he or Adam, which left the five men who they'd been sat with.

'You worry about getting better,' Colin said, squeezing her hand. 'And let us worry about the painting.'

The rest of the night passed in a flurry of activity.

Colin woke Adam up and made him go and get a doctor, who turned up quickly and checked on Maggie. Happy that no lasting damage had been caused, aside from the possibility of concussion, they helped her up off the floor and guided her to her bed. The doctor said he'd look after her, to make sure she stayed awake so that he could monitor her further.

Adam and Colin returned to their suite and Colin relayed what had happened, starting with the waking up and ending with the promise to investigate the missing painting.

Adam looked concerned.

'What is it?' Colin asked.

'Well, I'm supposed to be staying out of trouble.'

'An old lady has just been attacked and robbed, man,' Colin replied, barely keeping the disgust out of his voice.

'I know. Sorry. That was a stupid thing to say. Where do we start?'

4

BREAKFAST AND BLOODY MARYS

AFTER ALL THE excitement, Adam and Colin managed a few more broken hours sleep.

Upon waking, the first thing Adam noticed was the change in Colin. Usually, his best friend was easy-going and carefree, however, this morning he was charged and tense.

'What's up?' Adam asked.

'How could some scummy prick push an old woman over like that and steal from her? It's not right.'

Adam assumed that because Colin was the manager of a retirement home, a job he absolutely loved, he felt a certain affinity with poor Maggie. He was probably imagining someone doing the same to one of the old folks that he looked after.

'We'll find it,' Adam assured him. 'Luckily, there's only so many places someone can hide something on a boat. Even if this particular boat is bloody massive.'

They left their room and knocked on Maggie's door gently. The weary doctor answered and told them that Maggie was sleeping, and that he was pretty sure she wasn't concussed, but was staying with her to make sure she was safe. They thanked him, and told him they would return later.

They made their way down the stairs and into the food hall, the smells of fried eggs and succulent bacon causing their stomachs to growl with hunger. Having not eaten very much of the extravagant menu the previous evening, they piled their plates high with greasy breakfast food and sat down at a table.

Once their food had been eaten, and seconds had been collected, talk turned to the theft.

'At least the suspect pool is fairly narrow,' Adam said, shoving a fourth sausage into his mouth. 'Only five other people really knew about the value of the painting, and unless one of those five blabbed to someone else, and why would they, it has to be one of them.'

Colin nodded. 'Now we just need to figure out who.'

AFTER THEY'D FINISHED gorging themselves, they walked back up towards their room, where Maggie intercepted them.

She'd changed out of her pyjamas into a flowing black dress, a huge contrast from her multi-coloured garb from the night before. Her hair was pulled back into a tight bun and it looked as though she was in mourning.

'I just wanted to say thank you for last night,' she said, clutching Colin's arm.

'It's no problem at all,' he smiled. 'It's good to see you up and about. How are you feeling?'

'Okay. The back of my head is sore, but other than that and a few bruises, I'm right as rain. The doctor was a nice man and stayed with me to make sure I was grand. He said you called round on your way to breakfast.'

'We did. I know it's not the best time, but would you mind if we asked you a couple of questions?'

'Please do, though I'm not sure how much help I'll be.'

She ushered them into her suite and sat down on the sofa. Colin sat opposite her on the armchair while Adam lingered by the door like security.

'We won't keep you long,' Colin said. 'I was just wondering if anything had come back to you, about last night.'

'Sorry,' she said, shaking her head and wincing at the pain. 'Still the same. I opened the door, was pushed over, and woke up with you tending to me. You don't know how much that meant to me. Anything could've happened if it weren't for you.'

Colin waved the praise away. 'What about at dinner? Did anyone seem overly enamoured with the painting?'

'Well, the American was naturally interested in it, but that's his job. Once he examined it, he sat back down and conversation moved on. The well-to-do boy, the posh one, asked a few more questions about it, and I caught the others glancing at it every so often, but I guess that's only natural when you know how much it's worth.'

'No one asked about buying it or anything like that?'

'Lord, no,' she laughed. 'If all five of them bundled together, they still couldn't afford it. Well, maybe the actor could. It was valued at four million nearly ten years ago. Goodness knows what it's worth now.'

'And you've never thought about selling it?'

'Never,' she said, shaking her head. 'It has huge sentimental value, and I'd never considered selling it at any time of my life.'

'Thank you,' Colin said, getting up. 'We'll ask around and see what we can come up with.'

She pulled something from a handbag that was sitting beside her feet and tried to pass it to Colin.

'Your money is no good, here,' he said, pushing the notes back towards her and dismissed her protestations with a kind: 'Now, make sure you get some rest.'

They left her to it, with promises that they would update her with any developments. They walked back to their room to draw up their plan of attack, and quickly settled on locating one person.

THOUGH THE ELYSIAN was certainly big, thankfully it wasn't one of those ridiculous city-on-the-sea type affairs, and they managed to find Henry relatively quickly.

Despite the early hour, he was sat in the ship's casino, pushing coloured chips onto the roulette board. He was wearing a velvet smoking jacket, a crisp white shirt and a pair of tan chinos, and looked positively down in the dumps.

'Lady luck not smiling, eh?' Adam asked, as they approached him.

'You could say that. The pile doth diminish,' Henry half-smiled.

They watched the little white ball zoom around the roulette wheel, before bouncing and slowing, eventually settling in a red section. The croupier gave Henry a slightly pitying look as he raked up the remainder of the chips.

'And that's that, chaps,' Henry said, slapping his thigh and pushing himself up from the stool. They followed him to the bar, where he ordered the three of them a Bloody Mary each without asking, and led them to a table. The room was dark, and the small lamp on the table did little to alleviate that. When Henry spoke, it looked like he was doing that Hallowe'en trick of holding a torch underneath your chin.

'How are things, fellas?' he said. 'Enjoy dinner?'

'Not really my type of food,' Adam said.

'I quite agree,' nodded Henry. 'I thought it was okay, but when you've eaten fresh Beluga Caviar on the shores of the Caspian Sea, this mass-produced stuff like last night's fare pales in comparison.'

'Henry…' started Adam.

'Hazza. Please, call me Hazza. All my close friends do.'

'Okay. Hazza. You know Maggie?'

'Mmhmm, the old dear from our table last night?'

'Aye. Well, she was attacked last night in her room, and her painting was stolen. We were wondering if you knew anything about it?'

'That's bloody awful,' he gasped. 'She seemed like a spiffing sort.'

'She is,' Colin said. 'You don't happen to know anything about it, do you?'

'I'm hearing it for the first time from you, old sport. What could I possibly know about it?'

'We've heard that when we left the dinner last night, you were asking a few questions about the painting.'

'I did art history as a degree,' Hazza shrugged. 'In Florence, no less. I was simply interested in seeing a genuine masterpiece in the flesh. If showing an interest and making conversation is a crime, arrest me now.'

He held out his wrists and chortled.

'And where were you last night at three o'clock?' Adam asked, without humour.

'Chaps, forgive me if I'm gazing in the wrong direction here, but it seems to me like you are levelling accusations my way.'

'Not at all,' Adam said. 'We offered to help find the painting and naturally the people on our table from last night are the first people we're speaking to. We're simply trying to narrow down who could have taken it. Surely, you'd want to see the old lady reunited with her prized possession.'

'Obviously,' he said. 'Yes, obviously. Well, if you must know, I tried to chat up a waitress and failed spectacularly, so went back to my bunk alone.'

'And you stayed there all night?'

'Yes. All night, on my lonesome. Then, I woke up, showered, shaved, dressed and came straight here.'

'Did anyone at the table last night arouse your suspicions?' Adam asked.

'I think Tex is the only one, aside from myself, who understood the importance of the painting. The others probably saw a canvas and a gold frame and weren't that bothered, whereas I saw the effort, the love and all that comes with the creation of something special. Tex asked some questions about it, and obviously as an art dealer, he showed an interest in it, but nothing untoward.'

'Thanks for answering our questions, mate,' Colin said, before assuming a less authoritative air and gesturing to the roulette table. 'How much did you lose?'

'Oh, about a grand,' Hazza said. He tried to pass it off as if it wasn't very much, but Colin could see worry behind his eyes.

'Rough,' he said.

'Oh, luck comes and goes,' Hazza said, gazing around the room. 'Roulette wasn't my friend, but perhaps Blackjack will be. Now, if you'll excuse me, fellas.'

He patted them each on the shoulder two times, as if he'd learned his social cues from sleazy politicians, and strode off towards the card table with his chin in the air.

5

EBBS AND FLOWS

THE BOYS RETREATED to their room, and spent a while lounging about, discussing Hazza. The conclusion was that he either had too much money and didn't mind frittering it away in the name of fun, or that he was low on money and thought he could get a quick win on the roulette table to boost his balance. The latter seemed more plausible, considering the worried expression and the fact he was down a grand (at least) by eleven in the morning.

'I think Tex should be next on the list,' Colin said.

'Good shout,' Adam said. 'Let's go.'

'Hold up. I'm going to do some research on him first. Gimme ten.'

'That's why you're the best,' Adam said. 'I'm going to go and check in with Helena. See how she's getting on with that bloody dress.'

He went into his bedroom and closed the door, leaving Colin on the huge sofa. Colin pulled his phone from his pocket and searched for Tex Rivera. To his surprise, a rather official looking website for The Rivera Art Dealership appeared at the top of the page.

The background was black and the swirling logo for the company was tastefully rendered in silver. Below the banner, a photo of Tex standing beside a framed painting in a pristine gallery stayed for a few seconds, before being replaced by another very similar looking one. Different suit, different painting, same smug look. Colin imagined the wide smile was on account of the pretty penny he'd just made by flogging the painting he was standing in front of.

He found information on the company on one of the links. Tex had set it up a decade ago and had built it steadily, netting more than a million pounds in his first year and growing from there. It claimed he started the dealership out of his kitchen in San Antonio, Texas, before going global, with offices in no less than three continents.

It looked like things had been going well for Tex, right up until about three years ago.

On another page, there was a list of every painting Tex's company had been involved in the sale of. The entries were steady, and then seemed to dry up around 2019. Since then, only a handful of paintings had been sold, and even then, not for a lot. Certainly not enough to keep up what Colin imagined had been a lavish lifestyle.

'Adam!' Colin shouted, and his friend appeared.

'Got something?' he asked.

'I think I do.'

IT TOOK THEM a while to find Tex, but eventually, they did. He was reclining in a deck chair at the prow of the ship, his eyes hidden behind a pair of thick sunglasses. At first, Colin and Adam were unsure as to whether he was awake or not, and jumped when he spoke after a minute of them standing in front of them.

'Can I help you guys?' he drawled.

'Hi, Tex. It's Colin and Adam. We were at your table last night.'

'Right, right. Yeah, I remember. How are you guys doing?'

'We're alright,' Colin nodded. 'You mind if we sit?'

'Not at all,' Tex smiled. 'You want a drink?'

'We're fine for now, thanks.' Colin took a seat on one side of the American, and Adam sat on the other. Tex focussed his attention on Colin. 'You mind if we ask you a few questions about last night?'

'About what?'

'About Maggie's painting. It's gone missing.'

'No way,' Tex gasped. 'That's sad, man. She okay?'

'She's not taking it well,' Adam said. 'We're trying to help her.'

'Right on. That's good of you. Ask me anything, I'll do anything I can to help, too.'

Colin pulled a notebook from his pocket that he'd taken from the coffee table in their suite. At the sight of it and the Elysian embossed pen, Tex sat up a little straighter.

'You cops?' he asked.

Colin shook his head, suppressing a laugh. 'No, just a couple of do-gooders. But, we've found from experience that having notes of what people have said has come in handy. You don't mind, do you?'

'Of course not,' he said, though he looked like he didn't mean it.

'Can you tell us about last night?'

'You were there, man,' Tex said.

'We were, but it's good to hear events from a different perspective.'

'Okay. Well, I asked Maggie about the painting, had dinner and when Maggie left, Henry and I retired to a quieter bar for a nightcap.'

'Time?'

'Maggie left at about eleven. We all stayed at the table until midnight, then the others made their excuses. Henry, or Hazza as he insisted I call him, offered to pay for a decent brandy, and who am I to say no?'

'So you two went off to a bar. What time did you stay 'til?'

'We only stayed for one drink, and I was happily tucked up in bed by one thirty.'

'And Henry?'

'We left together. Far as I know he went to bed, too.'

'Did he try and chat up a barmaid?'

'He was trying to chat up anyone. Men like him, with money in the bank, think that's enough to pull whoever you want into the sheets.' There was disgust in his voice. 'Thankfully, everyone he tried said no.'

'Did you talk about the painting?' Colin asked.

'It came up,' Tex shrugged. 'Not every day you see something worth that amount of money.'

'What did you say about it?'

'I said nothing. Henry was asking the questions—was it really worth that much and who on earth would pay it? Those kinds of things. I told him it was definitely worth that much, and probably more than what poor Maggie thinks. Four million seems a bit low to me. As for who would buy it, there are art galleries and private collectors all over the globe who would pay that in a heartbeat.'

'And you have those connections?' Adam asked.

'Now, hold up. I hope that wasn't an accusation? Yes, I do have those connections, but purely professionally, you hear me, boy?'

Adam held up a pair of placating hands and nodded.

'I ain't got nothing to do with the theft, you hear?' Tex boomed again.

'We hear you. Adam didn't mean to make it sound accusatory, did you?' Colin said, and Adam shook his head.

'Fine,' Tex said, though he didn't look happy.

'Tell me about your business,' Colin said, trying to get back on to a level footing.

'Not much to tell. It's my baby, and I travel the world doing what I love. Not many people can say that.'

'I saw on the web that you've had a rough couple of years.'

'Ebbs and flows, my boy.' Tex smiled, but his words came out tersely. Colin could tell their chat was coming to an end. 'Truth is, art goes in waves. Sometimes, collectors fall over themselves to buy. Sometimes, it's like trying to sell ice to Eskimos. Or Inuits, or whatever you're supposed to call them now so as to not offend. What I'm saying is, you gotta plan for this. You have a bumper year, you be wise with your money. You hold on to some funds for when the lean year rolls around.'

Colin made to move, thinking Tex's business advice was the full stop in their conversation, but he was wrong.

'Matter of fact, this cruise isn't all for pleasure, it's for business, too. I've got an opportunity in Lisbon, when we stop tomorrow. I sell a painting there, I'm good for another couple of months. Like I say, ebbs and flows.'

6

LISBON, PORTUGAL

ADAM AND COLIN stood by the huge bedroom window, watching the City of Seven Hills grow larger as the ship was guided towards the port with military precision.

'So, you don't think we should try and get into his room?' Adam asked.

'I don't think so,' Colin shrugged. 'He's hardly going to tell us that he's going to sell a painting in the city, and it turn out to be the one taken from Maggie. If he was going to do that, he'd have kept schtum.'

'Yeah, you're probably right.'

Though frustrated with the lack of progress in the hunt for the missing art, Adam was excited about visiting a new city. He was Stonebridge born and raised, and had rarely ventured beyond the border of Northern Ireland, so he resolved to forget about their latest case while visiting Portugal's capital, and enjoy the city.

As the ship came to a halt, they grabbed their backpacks and made their way towards the gangplank.

AFTER TEN MINUTES of walking, the heat was stifling. Coupled with the vertiginous terrain, Adam was finding it tough to breathe. He motioned to Colin that he needed to sit down for a minute, and the two of them took solace on a nearby bench, bolted into the ground at a near forty-five degree angle.

'Why would anyone in their right mind build a city on such a hilly place?' Adam moaned.

'For the view?' Colin suggested, motioning to the expanse of ocean.

'Yeah, but at what cost? Everyone must be so knackered all the time that they can't be bothered to take in the view.'

'Not everyone is as unfit as you.'

'Shut up.'

As if to drive the point home, a little old lady with snow-white hair, marched past them while pushing a fabric shopping trolley. She smiled at them as she passed, and didn't look like a bead of sweat had been spilled with effort.

Adam jumped to his feet with renewed vigour, keen to show the show-off octogenarian that he could keep up, though they trailed in her wake as she made steady progress up the hill.

'Wow, you're really showing her,' Colin laughed.

Adam was too out of puff to even think of an appropriate rebuttal.

At the summit, they found themselves in a wide, cobbled courtyard. A couple of bars were welcoming their first customers of the day, while a line snaked out of a bakery and around the corner of the building.

'Beer or bread?' Colin asked.

'After that climb? Beer, I reckon,' said Adam.

They made their way to an outside table with a wide parasol that sheltered them from the blazing afternoon sun. They consulted a menu and, after a few minutes, a waiter in a casual shirt and a dainty fedora approached and took their order.

When their drinks had been deposited on the beermats in front of them, both Adam and Colin relaxed back in their seats and savoured the day. A light breeze blew through the square, and the frothy beer did a wonderful job of cooling them down further.

Talk turned to the wedding, and to Colin's own blossoming relationship. When they'd been growing up, they'd both been unlucky in love: unlucky in the sense that the opposite sex had generally considered them invisible. Now, things were looking up, and both were very positive about what was to come.

And then, ten minutes later, something stopped the conversation between them. Or rather, someone.

Tex Rivera, suited and with a tan Stetson perched atop his head, appeared over the brow of the hill. He was holding a large brown envelope. Sweat plummeted down his brow like a waterfall, and he walked with laser-like precision to the mouth of a street nestled between the bar and the bakery, eyes never once deviating from his course, and disappeared from view.

Adam jumped out of his seat and walked carefully to the lip of the street. He stood with his back against the stone building, and chanced a glance. The street was narrow, and opened onto a labyrinth of other smaller alleys and thoroughfares. Adam cursed, before quickly realising that they probably hadn't lost him at all. About a third of the way down the street was a small shop with a sign hanging above its door, proclaiming it to be the oldest art dealership in the country.

Adam hotfooted it back to the table, and relayed the information back to Colin.

'What do we do?' Adam asked.

'We wait.'

Adam ordered two more drinks, non-alcoholic this time, while Colin tinkered on his phone. It didn't take long for Tex to reappear, and when he did, he seemed to have an extra bounce in his step.

'Now what?'

'We go and visit the art dealer,' Colin said.

They quickly finished their drinks, left a tip on the table and made their way down the alley.

Muñoz Carvalho's shop looked small from the outside. The narrow window showcased a framed painting in the style of pointillism, and a carefully sculpted bronze figure that appeared to be mid-ballet move. It was tastefully done, to Adam's (very) untrained eye. Colin pushed the door open, and a little bell tinkling above their heads signalled their arrival.

A short, round man with weathered skin and a beautiful combover appeared from the back and greeted them warmly in English.

'Is it that obvious?' Adam laughed.

'Yes, my friend. You look like human milk bottle. Now, how may I help today?'

'I'm a huge art fan, and I've been looking forward to visiting your shop for many years,' Colin smiled, casting an admiring glance around the space.

The old man looked pleased.

Adam looked confused.

Colin continued. 'I've read about it, of course, in ARTnews. Quite a coup. The oldest shop in the city.'

'In all of Portugal,' the old man beamed.

'Of course, my mistake,' Colin said, marvelling at the four decorated walls. 'It's an honour to meet you, Mr Carvalho.'

'The honour is mine. Can I show you around?'

'Please.'

Muñoz showed an entranced Colin and a bemused Adam around his small shop, talking at length about the artwork that adorned the walls. He was passionate, and occasionally lapsed into rapid-fire Portuguese, before he corrected himself with an apology.

'Your English is very good,' Colin said, once all the paintings had been appraised.

'I work with dealers from all over the world. Middle-Easterns, Japanese...'

'American?' Colin interrupted.

'Sim,' he nodded.

'We just saw Tex Rivera out in the courtyard and we couldn't believe our eyes... well, I say we. This one,' Colin patted Adam's chest, 'wouldn't know the difference between a Picasso and a Pollock.'

Colin and Muñoz laughed heartily.

'Sim, Mr Rivera is a good man. He is respected in the art community for having a good eye. He bring me...'

The old man held a finger up and disappeared into the back.

'Oi, why are you making me sound like an idiot?' Adam hissed.

Before Colin could answer, the old man was back, holding a frame. He turned it to reveal a watercolour of snowy mountains and pink blossoms drifting from spindly trees.

'Glorious, no?'

'Yes, it's wonderful.'

'Like I say, Mr Rivera has good eye. It's not often a Kobayashi comes on the market.'

'Is that all he brought?'

'Sim. This is worth a lot of money. Though, he did mention that he has another painting that he had recently come into contact with, but he was saving it for one of the more renowned galleries in Venice.'

Adam and Colin exchanged a glance.

'Did he say anything else about it?'

'No, senhor. Just that it was out of my price range.'

Colin thanked him for the tour, and for his hospitality, before leaving his shop.

'When did you become a bloody expert on art?' Adam said.

'Took a quick Google crash course on Mr Carvalho while you were ordering the drinks. And good thing I did, too, because it looks like we have a lead.'

7

THERE'S NO BUSINESS LIKE
SHOWBUSINESS

ADAM AND COLIN sat in the first-class bar, sipping at a glass of expensive champagne that was entirely lost on both of them.

'Are you supposed to just know if it's good or not?' Adam asked. 'Tastes like paint stripper to me.'

'Not sure,' Colin replied, looking at the bubbles fizzing in the glass. 'Probably. I mean, not everyone can go to wine school or whatever it's called.'

'Maybe our taste buds have been wiped away from all the coke and crisps we've eaten.'

'Aye, or maybe we're just not cultured enough to appreciate the intricacies of such fancy drinks.'

'I barely know what the word intricacies means, so you're probably right.'

They clinked glasses anyway and downed the rest of the contents, much to the horror of an elderly couple who were watching on from a nearby table.

'So, what do you reckon then?' Colin asked.

'About Tex?'

'Aye.'

'Well, it seems pretty cut and dried. It looks like he's going to save the stolen painting for a more exclusive gallery in Venice, who can pay bigger bucks and who can probably provide a little more discretion.'

'But what if the painting he told Muñoz about wasn't the stolen one? It's just a better one than the one he sold in Lisbon.'

'The old man said that Tex told him that he'd recently come into contact with it,' Adam shrugged.

'That could've been a week before he boarded the ship.'

'So, what are you suggesting?'

'I think we should assume that Tex has the painting, and alert the Venetian authorities when we get a bit closer so that they can apprehend him upon arrival,' Colin said. 'However, I also think we should also make sure that we don't put all our chickens in one basket...'

'Eggs,' Adam interjected.

'Huh?'

'You put eggs in a basket, not chickens.'

'Is that what I said?' Colin laughed. 'Well, whatever nonsense I'm talking still stands. We focus on Tex, but make sure we keep an eye on the others too.'

'Why don't we just go all-out on Tex? Barge into his room, find the painting and all this ends.'

'Because you told me that you were supposed to be staying out of trouble,' Colin said. 'So, let's leave it to the authorities, who will catch him red-handed when he is trying to get off the boat with stolen goods. Meanwhile, let's try to enjoy ourselves.'

At that moment, the door to the bar flew open and in walked a smouldering Vaughn McClusky. He marched up to the bar and ordered a large glass of expensive whisky, before stalking off to a table near the back of the room where he sat with his head in his hands, long fingers scratching at his scalp.

'He looks troubled,' Adam said.

'Maybe we should go and lend a sympathetic ear,' Colin suggested.

'To the star of such hits as Dead In The Grave, Maximum Extermination and I'll Be Back Before I'm Dead?'

'Is that seriously the name of his biggest films?'

'Yeah.'

'No wonder he's not hit the big time yet!' Colin laughed. 'All I'm saying is, remember what we said about keeping our options open? You never know, he could have the painting safely stowed away in his room. This performance he's putting on could be a sign of guilt.'

'He's an actor, dumbass. If he'd stolen the painting, he'd be acting like he hadn't.'

'Could be double-bluffing.'

'You're an idiot,' Adam said. 'I know you want to help the old lady, so do I, but Vaughn is not our man. Though, because I'm a nosey so and so, I do want to know what's upset him.'

'Me too,' Colin said. 'Let's go.'

They picked up their drinks and sauntered across the room. As they approached him, Adam gazed at the actor's tailored blazer and fitted chinos, and wondered what it would be like to have enough money that nothing would ever be a worry again.

He asked Colin, who shrugged.

'Your worries become different, don't they?' he said, sagely. 'Instead of stressing about your next pay packet or mortgage payment, you probably start worrying about a stray grey hair or a deepening wrinkle. Show Business is a fickle game.'

'Goodness. I didn't realise I was talking to Aristotle!'

'I'm a font of knowledge,' Colin said. 'You should ask me big philosophical questions more often.'

'Will I ever be truly happy?' Adam asked.

'For a while next Saturday, aye, but then after that, naw. It's all downhill from the alter, my friend.'

They laughed as they weaved through the tables, though stopped as they came to Vaughn's. When he looked up, Adam noticed a vein popping in his forehead and blotchy marks under his eyes.

'Can I help you?' he asked.

'We were at the table with you the other night for dinner. Adam and Colin,' Adam said, waving his hands as a children's television presenter might, feeling like a prize idiot.

Colin grimaced, and took over. 'May we join you?'

Vaughn looked like he wanted to say no, but was probably imagining the headlines in Heat and The Daily Fail if a guest who was sitting close by ratted him out for not having time for his fans.

'Please, do,' he said, motioning to the seats.

'Quite a ship, eh?' Adam said.

'Yeah, it's big alright.'

'I've gotta say, I loved you in He's Behind You. It's about time the comedy detective genre was started up again, and you are the perfect man to get it going.'

'Thank you,' Vaughn said, graciously.

'Any plans for a sequel?'

'There's some talk of one, yes, but you never know in this business.'

'And what are you working on at the minute?' Adam asked.

'Well, I'm between projects, but I'm heading to Venice to have a chat with a producer about something big. Could be the one that takes me to the next level.'

'That's cool,' said Colin, trying to counteract Adam's over-the-topness by going the other way. 'You don't seem overly pumped by it. Is everything okay?'

'It will be. Hopefully. As with everything in this business, nothing is ever done until it's on a cinema screen. Right up until that moment, nothing is certain. Take this one, for example. The guy I'm going to meet thinks we have the funding to get started within the next three months. We have the hottest script in town, we have a director who has just won the best newcomer at Cannes, we've got a location with tax breaks. We have it all.'

'Except?'

Just then, Vaughn's phone beeped, and he instinctively reached a hand into his jacket pocket. From it, he produced one of those pill boxes that separate medication into days or doses, and popped two circular tablets from today's section. He threw them in his mouth and washed them down with the whisky.

'Probably a no-no,' he laughed. 'Sorry about that. What was I saying?'

'You were about to tell us why your next project isn't set in stone.'

'Oh yeah. We have it all, except the backing. The guy who was putting the money up dropped out this morning. He has "reservations", apparently,' Vaughn said, using his hands to make air quotes.

'And it can't get made unless he's on board?'

'Well, not necessarily him, but someone with money. We're talking multi-millions here. Not pocket money.' He took a hearty slug from his glass and wiped his top lip. 'I woke up this morning so bloody excited, and then he phoned. It's a soul-destroying business.'

'Something will come up, surely,' Colin smiled. 'Like you say, all the other pieces of the jigsaw are in place. Keep the faith.'

Vaughn smiled sincerely for the first time since they'd sat down. He reached out his hand and Colin shook it.

'You ever thought about going into life coaching?' Vaughn laughed. 'You'd make a bloody fortune in LA. Half the town would pay you a small fortune for the little pep talk you just gave me.'

'Now there's an idea,' Colin chuckled. 'Look, we've taken up enough of your time. We'll leave you to it.'

Vaughn thanked them, and as they walked away, he shouted after Adam.

'You're a fan, right?'

'Yeah.'

'I'm sorry for being a grump. Tomorrow night, let's have a proper drink and I'll be less of a dick. I promise.'

Adam nodded as casually as he could, but practically skipped from the room as soon as he was out of sight of the actor.

8

A BRIDGE OVER TROUBLED WATER

ADAM AWOKE THE next morning to the same shimmering sunshine, and the same stunning view of sea and sky. Yet this time, he found he wasn't enjoying it.

He checked the time, and was pretty sure that Colin would be up by now, so pulled on a T-shirt and a pair of shorts, and made his way into the lounge to find his friend reclined on the sofa, reading a book.

'Good morning,' Colin said.

'It's morning, but I don't know if it's a good one.'

'Oh, I don't know about that. We're in the middle of the ocean on a big old ship, en route to Barcelona where I thought we might pay a visit to the Nou Camp, and not long after that, we'll be in Venice and on to Lake Garda, and you'll be mumbling your vows to the woman you love.'

'Well, when you put it like that,' Adam smiled, and sat down on the other sofa. 'I just can't help thinking of poor Maggie, and it's sort of ruining the trip for me.'

'I know what you mean,' Colin nodded.

'So, I've got a plan.'

'Oh, no. I know that look.'

'What look?'

'That look in your eyes. You're going to suggest something that goes against everything you promised Helena before you left.'

'Yeah, but it's to help an old lady who has been robbed. And, if we can do that, the stress I'm feeling will disappear and I'll be able to enjoy the rest of the trip and the wedding.'

Colin stroked his chin. 'Tell me your plan.'

For the next few minutes, Adam talked and Colin listened, and when the talking was finished, Colin shook his head and said: 'That's insane.'

ADAM AGREED THAT the plan was insane. Of course it was.

But, he wanted this case to be over with, and so, desperate times called for desperate measures.

The boys got themselves dressed for the day and made their way down to breakfast. They grabbed a plate, filled it and sat down, casting their eyes around for their intended target, who was nowhere to be seen.

Unfazed, they began eating, discussing the finer points of the plan in hushed voices. Adam noticed Sean and Isiah, the two lads they hadn't managed to speak to yet, at a table by the door. They were laughing and joking like they had been pals for years, each clutching either an orange juice or a Mimosa. Probably the latter, Adam thought, judging by their joviality.

'We should chat to them at some point, too,' Colin said, following Adam's gaze. 'They look thick as thieves.'

Adam agreed.

Any further discussion on that point was cut off by the appearance of their man.

Tex Rivera.

He walked to the breakfast bar with the air of a man with the world at his feet. Despite the early hour, he was dressed to the nines; a gold blazer and crocodile skin loafers.

Adam gave him the thumbs up, and when he'd sorted his food, the art dealer made a beeline for their table. He sat down with a little groan, and greeted them with a firm handshake.

'What's with the get up?' Colin asked.

'Oh, this?' he said, pulling at one of the lapels. 'You know how Tiger Woods always wears a red tee on the final day of a tournament? Well, I always wear this the day after a big sale. It's become something of a tradition.'

'Ah, balls,' Adam said, suddenly. 'Do either of you have the time?'

'It's just gone eight thirty,' said Tex, checking an expensive Rolex.

'Sorry, gents. I'm going to have to love you and leave you for a minute,' Adam said, pushing himself up from the table. 'I said I'd phone Helena before she heads to work. Excuse me.'

Adam heard Colin mention a ball and chain, and Tex's raucous laughter followed him as he left the restaurant.

That's right, pal. Laugh it up, thought Adam as he made his way back to his room.

BACK IN HIS bedroom, Adam opened the door to the balcony. In the past twenty-four hours, he'd realised two things of note:

Firstly, the balcony doors could not be locked. Adam presumed it was to stop you locking yourself on the balcony, unable to get back into the room to contact help. It was a safety feature that was about to work to his advantage.

The second thing he'd noticed was that Tex's room was right next door to his.

Now, obviously they couldn't just knock on his door and ask for a look around. He was sure to close the door in their faces. But, a little nosey without supervision would surely yield results. So, Adam's plan was thus.

1. Climb from his balcony to Tex's
2. Have a look around the room
3. Uncover the stolen painting
4. Turn Tex over to the authorities at the next available opportunity
5. Enjoy the rest of the holiday

When he'd dreamt up his plan, the gap between the balconies had seemed smaller. Looking at them now, the chasm between them seemed comparable to the Grand Canyon. Coupled with the sheer drop, the frothing waves and deep blue sea below, not to mention the sharp-toothed things sure to be lurking down there, he felt terror stir in his bowels.

Literally.

He rushed back inside and made it to the toilet, just in time.

Back outside, he looked at the gap and wondered if he really cared this much? Was it worth putting his life on the line, and the happiness of his bride-to-be, just to get some stupid painting back?

Except, it wasn't just some stupid painting. It was a masterpiece. And, more than that—it was the very idea that someone thought they could take whatever they wanted, even if that something was from an elderly lady.

Buoyed, Adam tentatively climbed onto the railing, swung his leg over the wooden handrail and reached out, ever so carefully, towards Tex's balcony.

Suddenly, the boat lurched sideways as it crested a wave, and Adam felt for sure that he was a goner. He gripped onto the rail with all his strength, his knuckles white from the effort of clinging on, and when the boat righted itself, found that he was still alive.

As quickly and as carefully as he could, he clambered over the top of the balcony and fell onto the ivory tiles on his back, panting with exertion and relief. He took a few minutes to compose himself, before getting up and making his way into Tex's room.

It wasn't quite up to the same standard as the Bridal Suite, but it wasn't far off. Adam surveyed the space, cursing the fact that the painting wasn't there in the centre of the room, propped on an easel with a spotlight focussed on it.

No, that would be *far* too easy.

Instead of wallowing, and aware that his time alone was running out, he tore through the main room and the bedroom like a Tasmanian Devil. He scooped up the sheets to check under the bed, he checked behind the sofa and in the kitchen cupboards, but came away empty handed.

And then he realised where it would be.

In Adam's own bedroom—or cabin he supposed it was called on a ship—there was a huge safe concealed within the wardrobe. In Tex's room, the same turned out to be true. Behind the wardrobe's mirrored door, sat a metal box with a small digital display and a keypad. It was built so ruggedly that it looked like a stick of dynamite would barely make a singe mark.

Adam supposed that there was nothing else for it.

He didn't want to guess the code, in case the police who investigated dusted the place for prints. He realised that he'd touched other places in the room, but surely they wouldn't be dusting the bottom of a valance.

Reluctantly, he slid the wardrobe closed again and made his way out of the room. At the door, he cast one last glance back, before slinking out, content at hearing it click locked behind him; but frustrated that he'd left the American's room empty handed.

9

LUCKY'S

ADAM AND COLIN cut frustrated figures as they sat on the sofa in their suite, facing each other.

'In reality, it doesn't change much,' Colin shrugged. 'Does it?'

'I guess not,' Adam said, though the disappointment of not finding the painting was etched on his face. He'd been looking forward to bringing the case to a close and getting on with his pre-wedding trip. 'Tell me again what you chatted about.'

'Nothing, really. He told me about selling the painting in Lisbon...'

'And you didn't ask about the one he plans to sell in Venice?'

'How could I?' Colin said. 'If he knew that we knew that, he'd know we were snooping around after him.'

'True. Good point, well made. What else?'

'Future plans. I told him about you getting married, he told me that he's going to fly home from Italy and spend some time with his family.'

'And he didn't seem on edge, or anything?'

'No,' Colin said, shaking his head. 'Cool as a cucumber. Made me doubt our hypothesis a bit, actually.'

'You don't think it's him?'

'I don't know. But I think we should get on with chatting to the others. We've spoken to Hazza, Tex and Vaughn, which leaves two more.'

'Sean and Isiah.'

'Indeed. So, I'm thinking we head out for a walk and see if we can bump into either of them. See if they know anything.'

'Plan. Gimme ten,' Adam said, and made for the bedroom.

ADAM PLUGGED HIS phone into the charger and waited for it to power up. He thought that chatting to the other two cold would be a waste of time, but maybe with a bit of information about them, the conversations could yield some results. (He'd been impressed when Colin had done it before entering the art gallery in Lisbon, and wanted to be similarly prepared.)

When the phone flashed, he snatched it up and opened Safari. He typed in Isiah's name, and was dismayed by the lack of results. It appeared that Isiah was like Adam, and was staying in first class by the grace of God (or thanks to the kindness of a family member). There was no evidence to link him to a famous family, or a business, or a won fortune.

Unlike Sean O'Connell, who it transpired was the son of an Irish businessman called Trevor.

Adam read an interview on the Financial Time's website, all about how Trevor's business was dealing with the fallout from Brexit. Amongst the doom and gloom of export prices and European red tape, there was a little golden nugget.

It appeared that Trevor thought Sean was an unsuitable candidate to take over the running of the business when the time came. Apparently, Sean did not possess the business acumen required to step into the role of heir apparent. When pushed, Trevor had hinted that his son wasn't good at budgeting, before moving the interview on.

Adam set the phone down and thought about what that meant. Could his father's public ire and disappointment have turned Sean into a thief? Had he stolen the painting in the hope of selling it on, and showing his father just how good he was with money?

It seemed a bit far-fetched, but that was where they were. Adam left his phone where it was, filled Colin in with what he had found, and set off in search of their prey.

IT TURNED OUT Sean was to be located relatively easy. They found him slouched over a bar, though not in the first-class lounge.

Lucky's was an Irish-themed pub in the middle of the boat. The décor was tacky, as if the person in charge had googled "Irish themed pub" and ordered anything and everything that they'd seen. Bunting with pots of gold and leprechauns hung overhead, green bulbs bathed the room in a sickly glow, and antique Guinness signs were plastered over every available surface.

As Colin and Adam took a seat on either side of Sean, The Dropkick Murphy's "I'm Shipping Up To Boston" gave way to "Dirty Old Town" by The Pogues, perhaps setting the tone for their chat.

Sean pushed his fiery red curls behind his ears and assessed his guests with bleary eyes.

'Right, lads?' he asked.

Adam nodded and introduced them both, in case Sean had forgotten who they were, or was too inebriated to remember.

'I remember ye, alright. Ye fancy a drink?'

'We're grand, thanks.'

'Suit yoursels,' he said, downing the remainder of his pint and motioning to the bartender for another. 'If ye don't want a drink, what are ye after?'

He said it with a smile, but the words seemed barbed.

'Well, it's a bit of a sensitive subject, actually. Do you mind if we have a chat somewhere a bit more private?'

Sean nodded and pointed towards a booth at the far side of the room. He waited for his pint while Adam and Colin got settled on the bench seats. They watched as Sean stumbled towards them, taking care not to lose a single millilitre of his stout.

'Right ye are,' he said, gulping down a third of his pint, before jutting his chin in their direction. 'Hit me.'

'Right,' Colin said. 'Remember the first night where we all had dinner?'

'Aye.'

'Do you remember the old woman?'

'I do. Bit mad, wasn't she?'

'A bit,' Colin conceded. 'Well, she's had her painting stolen, and we're looking to get it back. We're asking all the people from the dinner table if they know anything.'

'First I'm hearing of it, if I'm honest. I feel bad for the lady, but what do you expect is gonna happen if you parade a priceless painting about? Bit of a mad move if you ask me.'

'You haven't heard anything or seen anything suspicious?'

'Like I said, first I'm hearing about it.'

Colin looked disappointed.

'How are you affording being in first class?' Adam asked, suddenly.

'What did you say to me?' Sean said, all affability gone. His teeth were bared and the stink of stout clouded the space between them.

'It's just…'

'I know what you're about to say. You've read that bloody article that my dad did, slagging me off to high heaven about my spending. Let's not get things twisted here—he's right. I'm pap with money. Always have been, always will be. As soon as I get paid, I'm straight to the nearest bar or shop or what have you, and it's gone before I know it. I'm too generous for me own good.'

'So…'

'So how am I here? In a turn up for the book, old Daddy O'Connell paid for it. And it's not his way of saying sorry, neither. Don't you go thinking he's soft. I'm here for work. On a "networking mission" apparently.' He made air quotes with grubby fingers and necked the rest of his pint. 'Daddy told me to get to know people, look for investment opportunities or, more to the point, someone that would take me off his hands.'

'What do you mean?'

'He wants me involved in his company as much as I want this latest batch of crabs.' He pointed to his belt. 'I'm here to further his business interests, and if I can sweet talk someone into taking me on, then all the better.'

'So you and your dad aren't the best of friends? What happens if he does cut you off?' Adam asked.

'Then I'm out on me ear.'

Adam and Colin shared a glance.

'No, no, no,' Sean shouted. 'I'm not having you two wee pricks thinking that my possible lack of income means that I was desperate enough to steal that wee woman's painting. Money might burn a hole in my pocket when I have it, but I'm no thief. I'd rather live on the streets than take something that isn't mine, especially from an old lady.'

To Adam's ears, it seemed convincing.

'And if you're pointing fingers at anyone, I'd have a look at that Isiah fella. I've only known the guy a few days, and he's already tried to get me involved in some of his get-rich-quick schemes. I imagine he couldn't believe his eyes and ears when that dotty old lady brought her priceless art to dinner!'

10

THE PROPHET

AS IF THE day hadn't yielded enough excitement, there was another black-tie dinner affair to attend.

With knowledge of what the evening would hold, Adam and Colin headed off to the KFC on board and loaded up on chicken wings and chips. They discussed the type of person who would slather their meal in the Colonel's special gravy, and came to the conclusion that it was the work of a psychopath.

Then, talk turned to more serious matters.

Tonight's dinner would give them the chance to be in the room with all of the suspects once more, presuming that they were planning to attend. It was assumed that table arrangements would not be the same as the opening evening, and so they divvied the persons of interest up.

Colin would keep an eye on Sean and Vaughn. Easy to remember because it rhymed.

Adam would shadow Tex, Hazza and Isiah, the only person they had not yet spoken to about the missing painting.

Bellies full, they headed back up the stairs to their room, stopping off at Maggie's on the way. When she answered the door, they barely recognised her. It was as if her skin was shrinking, pulling it tight to her skeleton, exposing each and every bone.

'Hi, boys,' she said, her voice sounding like she'd smoked a thousand cigarettes since she'd last seen them.

'Hi, Maggie,' Colin said. 'We just wanted to check if you wanted a couple of handsome, muscular men to accompany you to dinner tonight?'

'We thought we'd call early enough that if you say yes, we've got time to go and find them,' Adam joked.

A small, brittle smile formed on her face, but only for a second. The sadness that she was feeling was plain to see.

'That's very kind of you, but I'm not going. The thought of being in the same room as the thief and scoundrel who took my beloved painting is too much to bear.'

'Perfectly understandable,' Colin nodded. 'We just wanted to let you know that we're still asking around. We promised that we'd find it, and we're not giving up.'

'You are good boys,' Maggie said, patting them on their arms. 'Your mummies must be so proud.'

With that, she bade them a soft goodbye and closed the door.

'Poor Maggie,' Adam said, as they headed to their own room.

Inside Colin, the fire to get the painting back grew even stronger.

COLIN AND ADAM appeared in the plush dining room wearing the same clothes as the first night. The same people looked at them with the same disgust. Adam was even sure that the pianist was playing the same song as he had been the first night—though, of course, one piece of classical music sounded the same as the next one in his mind. It was a bit like Groundhog Day.

Keen to keep a clear head, they grabbed a couple of soft drinks from the bar and chose a seat near the door, figuring everyone who came or went would have to walk past them.

Over the course of the next half an hour, nearly all of the players arrived. Hazza and Vaughn arrived a few minutes apart, both in very expensive suits. A short while later, Isiah entered the room with a very drunk looking Sean on his arm. There was no sign of Tex.

Adam was unsure if he was being paranoid, but he thought that Isiah had given them a dirty look as he'd entered.

Had Sean given him a heads-up that Adam and Colin would be looking to have a word with him?

Surely not, Adam thought. If Sean was so close to Isiah, he probably wouldn't have blabbed about his get-rich-quick ideas to them earlier in the day. He watched as Isiah led Sean to the bar, and heard them squabbling as the former tried to order the latter a soft drink. After much consternation, the Irishman stumbled off clutching a pint of lager, leaving Isiah to pay the bill.

The evening passed much as the last had. Edd, the captain, gave another speech, welcoming the first-class guests, as well as those from other parts of the ship who had splashed out on a ticket to the black-tie event. Adam was surprised that he left out his "going overboard" joke for the new faces in the room.

The assembled were asked to find a seat, and Adam was sure that their suspects made a point of scampering quickly to tables in the far reaches of the room-as far away from he and Colin as possible.

Small talk and introductions were made, the food came (squid ink soup for starters, duck heart with an assortment of odd vegetables for main) of which Adam once again ate absolutely nothing, grateful for the lasting fullness courtesy of Colonel Sanders. The others at the table were aghast when Adam returned his plate, practically untouched. He heard the mother and daughter, sitting opposite, muttering about how money changes people, and that there were poor folk on the street who would do disgraceful things for a morsel of that food that had been so unthoughtfully discarded.

Adam was about to answer them back, to tell them that he was as far from rich as it was possible to be, when something out of the corner of his eye caught his attention.

Isiah was weaving his way through the tables, headed for the door while typing a message on his phone.

'Make sure no one takes my dessert while I'm away,' Adam said, pushing himself out of his seat. 'It's the only part of the meal I have any hope for.'

'No worries,' Colin shouted after him.

As Adam crossed the floor, Isiah turned his head and cast a look around. Adam tried to act naturally and pretended that, instead of following him, he was on the way to the bar. He didn't acknowledge Isiah's nod.

When the door had closed behind his quarry, Adam gave it ten seconds and then followed suit. For a second, Adam couldn't see Isiah and thought he had blown his chance, but then he caught sight of his distinctive hairdo a little way down the deck and proceeded to tail him carefully.

Not that care was needed. Isiah was seemingly on a mission.

From Adam's point of view, it looked like he was trying to recreate the video of The Verve's seminal Bittersweet Symphony video. If someone was in Isiah's way, he simply shouldered into them, creating a path and never deviating from it. He got some dirty looks on the way, but was oblivious to them. As Adam passed the disgruntled victims, he heard Isiah called a few choice names. None of which Adam could disagree with.

He watched Isiah turn into a bar called Ricardo's. Adam sidled up to the window and peered in. It looked like a classy enough joint. Leather upholstered booths lined three of the walls, with the fourth taken up by a long, marbled bar with an array of drinks behind it. A barman in a tight shirt and waistcoat threw a thousand-watt smile in Isiah's direction as he took his drink order, probably in the hope of a hefty tip.

Adam watched Isiah lift his glass and walk to a booth currently inhabited by a woman with long, dark hair and a Mediterranean complexion. She smiled as he edged into the seat opposite her, his back to Adam, and leaned across the table to kiss her cheek.

Adam took his chance and ran to the booth that backed on to Isiah's. Thankfully, there was a wooden divide between the booths that afforded Adam some secrecy. He listened to Isiah and the girl make small talk for a while and watched in horror as a barman walked across the room, zeroed in on his table. Quickly, he grabbed a menu and pointed to a cocktail, hoping that the employee might mistake him for a mute. The barman nodded his head, noted down his order and walked away without a word.

Adam let out a sigh of relief, before going back to his covert surveillance.

And just in time, it would seem. The girl, who was called Marianne, was speaking.

'Can I come back with you?'

'There's no point,' Isiah said. 'The party is nearly over, and I'd have to buy you a ticket.'

'Oh.'

'It's not that I don't want to take you,' he placated. 'I just mean it would be better if you came to the next one, so that you can taste the food and hear the captain speak and stuff. It's an experience.'

'Is it expensive?'

'Yeah, but don't worry about that. I'll get you a ticket.'

'Last night you said that you didn't have a lot of money, though. I'm happy to pay.'

'Honestly, don't worry about it. I have a good thing going when we land in Barcelona.'

'A good thing?'

'Not for you to worry about.'

'Money?'

Silence. Adam supposed Isiah must've nodded, because Marianne's question sounded like a follow up.

'Enough to get me a ticket for the next party?'

Isiah laughed. 'If all goes to plan, enough to buy a yacht of our own.'

11

BARCELONA, SPAIN

COLIN'S TWO EXPERIENCES of Barcelona were as disparate as they came.

Firstly, like many men his age, he'd grown up mesmerised by its football team. Year after year, Messi and co had torn through the Champions League, thrashing minnow and monolith alike, while playing some of the most beautiful football the world had ever seen.

His second involvement with the Catalan city was second-hand through his grandad. It was a story that was brought out every Christmas day when sat around the table, much to the delight of everyone (aside from his grandad—Derek—who would busy himself with the gravy).

Fifteen years or so ago, when Colin was still in primary school, Grandad McLaughlin had travelled to the Spanish city for a weekend away. Usually softly-spoken and agreeable, he had spent a whimsical weekend away with his wife of thirty-seven years. They'd seen the sights, eaten local delicacies and perused the world-famous art that was housed in the city's many galleries.

They'd had a whale of a time.

On the final morning, they'd left their hotel looking for a spot of breakfast. Deciding on a picturesque café on La Rambla, they took a seat at one of its tables, sheltered from the morning sunshine by a large, lager-branded parasol. They ordered their food without looking at the menu, and waited.

And waited.

When a waiter walked past them, Derek engaged him politely, enquiring where their food was. The waiter marched off towards the kitchen and returned to tell them their huevos rancheros would be along shortly, and strode off again without apology.

Derek detested rudeness, but let it slide. He'd heard some nasty stories about finding all sorts in the food of those who complained, and was keen to have a completely sanitary meal.

Fifteen minutes later, the food was plonked down in front of them on plastic plates. The experience thus far was not living up to his vision, but he kindly put it down to a rumbling tummy and low blood pressure. He was sure that once the food touched his tastebuds, the lateness of the food and the insolence of the staff would soon be forgotten.

He was wrong.

The food was cold and inedible.

He summoned the same waiter again and complained. The waiter sighed and offered to get him another plate, though Derek refused. He reasoned things would not get better at this café, and got up to leave. The waiter held up a finger, and walked off. Mr McLaughlin imagined he'd gone to get the manager to come and apologise for such a nightmare scenario, and decided he'd accept with good grace, not wanting to end the holiday on a sour note.

The waiter returned alone, and sat the bill down on the table in a small metal platter. Mr McLaughlin laughed, thinking it a joke, and gathered his things. The waiter blocked his way and pointed at *la cuenta*, insisting he hand over the required amount of euros.

Things almost came to blows, when a passing police officer came to the rescue. He listened to both of their arguments, and though he sided with the Northern Irishman, insisted that the café be paid. They *had* made the food, after all.

Despite their flight not leaving until six in the evening, Grandad McLaughlin dragged his wife to the airport at 11:30am, insisting that he did not want to spend one more minute in a city filled with bent coppers and filthy, thieving scoundrels. He saw out the rest of the day with a Jack Reacher book, scowling at anyone who dared look slightly Spanish.

The experience had scarred him so, he'd never returned to mainland Europe.

Still, despite the cautionary tale, Colin was excited about visiting Spain's second city.

Or, he had been. He'd been looking forward to squeezing as much in as he could. A visit to the hallowed turf of the Nou Camp; climbing the many steps inside the Sagrada Familia, and seeing the artwork of Barcelona's most famed architect—Antoni Gaudí.

Instead, he was now planning on tailing Isiah Lookman to an art gallery, where hopefully he would try and flog the stolen painting, meaning Colin and Adam would have their evidence, and the whole debacle would be sewn up by the time they left port that evening.

He sighed, picked up his backpack and made his way out of the breakfast room as the city grew nearer, the ship slowing to begin its crawl to the quayside. Colin marvelled at the steady hand it took to guide a 100,000 tonnes of cruise liner into what was essentially a parking space!

Colin and Adam stationed themselves near the ship's exit, hoping to catch sight of Isiah so that they could tail him. As the ship came to a halt with the smallest of bumps, the crew launched into action and in no time at all, the gangplank was set and a crowd armed with DSLR cameras and Lonely Planet guide books disembarked in an orderly fashion.

Eventually, they spotted Isiah. He was dressed smartly: pressed shirt and tie, suit trousers, with a pair of Ray-Ban style shades perched atop his nose. On his back was one of those bags people take when they go hiking.

Adam nudged Colin, 'That bag is plenty big enough to be hiding the painting.'

'Agreed,' Colin said.

They watched him cast glances left and right, before smiling at the employee who was standing at the top of the steps and making his way down them. Colin and Adam gave him a head start and then followed.

They trailed him through the bustling streets, trying to keep their eye on him, while ignoring the beautiful sights the city had to offer. They tailed him to a swanky bar that was just opening its doors. He took a seat at an outside table, while Adam and Colin entered a bookshop across the street. From here, they watched him through the shop window, while pretending to peruse the books, which were mostly written in Spanish.

Isiah looked nervous.

Adam remembered the confidence and swagger with which he'd spoken to the girl from last night; how, after today's deal, he'd be rich enough to take her wherever she wanted in the world.

That self-assurance seemed to have deserted him. He looked around like a lost child and checked his phone every ten seconds or so. He nearly fell out of his chair when the waiter approached with his drink.

'What do we do?' Adam asked.

'We wait, I guess,' Colin replied.

'You don't think we should go and get the policia?'

'I think we let him sell the painting, then make our move. That way, we have concrete evidence that he has done something illegal. If we go now, he could say something like he was getting it valued for her as a surprise, or something.'

So, they waited.

The shopkeeper approached them in a friendly manner, and they told him they were just looking, while pretending to read the blurb of a book called 'Suburbio.'. After fifteen minutes of "just looking", the shopkeeper took exception, motioning to the door and muttering 'no es un biblioteca.'

Thankfully, Isiah was wrapped up enough in his own thoughts to notice a shifty looking Adam and Colin scrambling out of the bookshop and spilling into the perfume shop next door.

The conflicting aromas and overpowering scents made Adam's head hurt the moment they were through the door, though mercifully, across the plaza, Isiah jumped as his phone vibrated on the table. He read whatever the text said, downed the rest of his beer, and stood.

Adam and Colin followed him, taking care to avoid one of Isiah's many paranoid glances. At the end of the street was a small art gallery. Adam took out his phone, ready to snap a picture of the rogue dealer entering the shop. Isiah stopped by the window, and spent a minute or two looking at the canvases on display, before taking a step forward and disappearing down the alley at the side of the shop.

'What's he doing?' Adam asked.

'Not sure,' Colin said, already making his way over. 'Maybe there's a back door?'

They strode across the street, and hooked their heads around the entrance to the alley. There, at the far end, was Isiah. He was talking to a shifty looking man, who was peering into the gaping opening of the backpack. The man nodded, and Isiah looked relieved. The man reached into his pocket, shuffling his hand around like he was trying to take hold of something.

Suddenly, he produced a little silver whistle and blew it. All of a sudden, the alleyway was teeming with police officers. They rushed from both sides of the narrow lane, almost knocking Colin and Adam into the gutter. Two grabbed Isiah and slammed him against the wall, slapping handcuffs around his wrists. One opened the bag and lifted out a huge block of cocaine, wrapped in cling film and held together with duct tape, and showed another officer.

Adam and Colin watched as the rest of the bag was emptied, and left when it was clear that there was no painting.

Their suspect pool had just dropped by one.

12

A MULTITUDE OF UNEXPECTED
EVENTS

THE NEWS OF Isiah's arrest passed around the ship like wildfire, and Colin noticed at dinner that night that most of their suspects were keener than usual to keep their distance from he and Adam.

They were only two days out from Venice, and if they didn't find the painting soon, Colin knew that it would be gone for good. They had to step up their game.

At a table in the corner of the room, they discussed what their next step was. Perhaps it was time to go nuclear—ask the captain to search rooms or implore him to make an unscheduled stop into the nearest port so that the police could intervene.

That was perhaps the most sensible plan, but Colin had a burning desire to be the one who took down the thief. Images of poor Maggie, unconscious on her cabin floor kept surfacing in his memory, and he knew he couldn't hand the reins over to someone else. Not yet. Not while there was still the chance to catch the bastard themselves.

As frustration pooled, they once more went over the suspects.

Vaughn had a film he really wanted to make, and the producer had backed out. Could he have stolen the picture to cover the lost money? Adam's counter-argument was that he probably had enough money in his wallet right now to fund his passion project, without having to steal. Hell, he'd been paid almost ten million for his last film. He was hardly in need.

However, Sean *was* in need. Cut off from the family business and here on the boat in the hope of gaining employment. It was a highly embarrassing situation to be in, especially after being publicly mocked by his own flesh and blood. Surely, the lure of an easy four million (at least) was reason enough to steal the painting.

Hazza was in a similar position. On the first night, he had hinted that his family thought him an idiot, frittering away his grandfather's inheritance by leading a playboy lifestyle. The chance to show them that he wasn't such a plonker must be tempting, and returning home from a lavish holiday with the news that he was no longer dependent on their cash was a pretty nice incentive.

'I still can't see past Tex,' Adam said. 'He has the most skin in the game. Art is his thing.'

'Yeah, but imagine selling the painting and not being able to tell anyone. From his website, it seems that the prestige is half the reason he's in the game at all.'

'Aye, but I can think of at least four million reasons why he might keep his mouth shut. You heard him. Ebbs and flows, and this painting is probably enough to say goodbye to rainy days for a good old while.'

'So what do you suggest?' Colin asked.

Adam's suggestion would have to wait, as Vaughn McClusky had appeared at their table. He beamed at them, holding a tray with three glasses of amber liquid.

'Gentlemen,' he said, 'I hope I'm not interrupting anything, but I felt like I should both apologise and thank you for the other night.'

He passed a glass to Adam.

'Firstly, an apology to you. I was in a foul mood when we spoke last. I'm in a very fortunate position where I can act for a living, and I wouldn't be in this position with support from wonderful people like you. Secondly,' he passed Colin his drink, 'a thank you. After your pep talk, I got off the pity train and mobilised. Like I said, I'm in a fortunate position, and I have total confidence that this film will be a success, so thanks to your advice, I've decided to put up the money myself. When we get to Venice, I'm meeting the producer on his yacht to iron out the details, but without your wise words, that probably wouldn't have happened.'

He held his glass aloft and they all clinked together, before sipping at the whisky. Colin knew that Adam had never been into that particular drink, as he felt the burn in the throat was more akin to torture, but today he was acting like he bloody loved it.

'Now,' Vaughn said. 'Ask me anything.'

For the next half an hour, drinks flowed and so did conversation. Adam was in his element, ohh-ing and ahh-ing as he found out juicy details from behind the scenes, Vaughn's future plans and a unique insight into the actor's much publicised battle with a life-threatening illness almost a decade ago.

'Let me ask you a question,' the actor said. 'How is Maggie? I've not seen her about.'

'I don't think anyone will until we hit port. She's taken it very hard.'

'Makes my blood boil,' Vaughn replied. 'Are you still looking into it? Any theories?'

Adam told him about his hunch—that Tex was behind it. They scanned the room, to discover that, once again, he hadn't shown his face at dinner. To Adam, this was further evidence of his wrongdoing. He was keeping away in the hope that he could make it off the ship without being questioned again.

'Why don't we get the captain to open up his room?' Vaughn said. 'Surely, a quick search would clear this whole thing up.'

'We could, I suppose,' Colin shrugged.

'And no time like the present,' Vaughn said, rising to his feet and throwing the rest of the expensive whisky down his throat.

THE CAPTAIN WAS shocked and appalled that a theft had taken place on his ship, and that he was only finding out about it now. He told them in no uncertain terms that had he known about it from the moment it had happened, Maggie would have been reunited with her artwork a long time ago. He snatched a skeleton key card from his office and marched with them through the ship towards Tex's room.

The captain strode in front, a man on a mission, with Vaughn on his heels. Adam and Colin struggled to keep up.

'Should we tell Maggie, first?' Adam asked.

'I don't think so,' Vaughn replied, looking back over his shoulder without breaking pace. 'If things get violent, we want her out of harm's way.'

Colin almost laughed at the way Vaughn had delivered the line. Adam, on the other hand, loved it. He knew that the situation was terribly serious, but the fact that he was part of something that resembled a Vaughn McClusky movie was not lost on him.

They descended staircases and brushed past people who looked on agog.

When they got to Tex's cabin, they stopped in a line, pressed against the wall. Captain Edd knocked briskly on the door and shouted the occupant's name.

There was no answer.

He held his ear against the door and narrowed his eyes, straining to hear movement from inside.

'Mr Rivera, I'm coming in,' he shouted, and pressed the key card against the shiny sensor to the side of the door, causing the little light to turn from red to green. The door clicked open and swung inwards ever so slightly.

Edd pushed lightly, and stepped over the threshold. Vaughn went next, and before Colin or Adam could follow, they heard the captain shout a few choice words.

The reason for his expletives quickly became apparent.

13

THE CONTENTS OF TEX'S CABIN

COLIN FOLLOWED VAUGHN into the room, so close behind him it felt like a parachute jumper leaving a plane in a war movie. Perhaps he was getting carried away, what with being in such close proximity to the actor.

Adam was less keen to enter the room. The captain's oaths had shaken him, and he hoped that the cause of the shouts was simply the discovery of the painting, though something within him knew different.

He rounded the corner, shoulders scraping against the doorframe, eyes partially covered by shaking hands, to be confronted with…

Nothing.

Slowly, he removed his fingers from in front of his eyes and glanced around. There was nothing out of place. As when he had come on his little covert operation, there was no painting, no easel, no hint that anything was wrong.

And then he looked over to where Edd, Vaughn and Colin were standing. They were peering into the bedroom with ashen faces. Adam took a step towards them.

'Mate,' Colin said, 'I don't think you'll be able to handle it.'

'Shut up,' Adam replied, not wanting to lose face in front of Vaughn. 'Whatever it is, I'm sure I'll be grand.'

Colin shrugged and moved out of the way, letting Adam take his place.

One glance at the scene was enough to send Adam running for the open door, where he hurled his guts over the ledge and into the frothing sea below. He knew that what he had just seen would be etched into his brain until his dying day.

The open en-suite door.

Tex's body in the bath.

The blood.

Adam heaved again, his stomach cramping and his throat burning with the bile that came in torrents.

He felt a soft pat on his back, and took a moment to regain his composure. Using his sleeve, he wiped gunk from his chin and turned to find Vaughn looking at him with sympathy.

'I feel the same, mate. Bloody horrific,' he said. 'Edd's going to stay with the body. He's asked me to go and tell his second-in-command, so that they can phone ahead to Venice and have the police on standby. You want to come with me?'

Adam considered it, and then shook his head.

'No worries,' Vaughn said, tapping him twice on the chest before rushing off.

Colin appeared a few minutes later, his face white; his expression a far-off stare. He leaned on the railing beside Adam, and neither of them said anything for a very long time.

Finally, Adam spoke.

'Do you know what happened?'

'There's a note.'

'A note? What, like he did that to himself?' Adam repeated. 'Jesus. What did it say?'

Colin pulled out his phone, navigated to the photo album and passed it to Adam, whose eyes flitted wildly about the screen, trying to take in all the details at once, but finding it hard to concentrate.

He closed his eyes for a few seconds, and when he opened them, it seemed they were ready to follow his orders. He read from the start of the letter.

> *I couldn't live with the guilt. That poor old woman. It was a moment of madness, and I couldn't live with myself any more. Cracthen is at the bottom of the sea. I couldn't bear to give it back—couldn't bear to see Maggie's disgust, so I tossed it overboard in the middle of the night. I've robbed the world of a masterpiece, but*

I've robbed a family of something worse. Tell her I'm
sorry. I'm so, so sorry.

Tex

Adam re-read the letter a few times before passing the phone back to his friend, just as Vaughn reappeared with a couple of the crew.

'Boys, we're no use here anymore. Let me buy you a drink.'

They nodded and followed the actor to the nearest bar, where he bought a round of beers. They toasted the painting, and they toasted Maggie, who would be heartbroken when she found out about her masterpiece's fate.

They had one more after that, though Adam could see that Colin wanted to be elsewhere. When Vaughn offered another round, they declined and parted company.

'You okay?' Adam asked Colin as they walked back to their cabin.

'Not really,' he said, and Adam knew he was thinking about poor Maggie.

The rest of the journey was spent in silence. Tex's door had red tape across it, and a crew member standing to the side, presumably to keep an eye on it until they reached Venice, and so that an unsuspecting maid wouldn't have to encounter what was behind the door, should she stumble into the room mistakenly.

As soon as they got back to their room, Colin collapsed onto the sofa and put a cushion over his face. Adam sat opposite, quietly, letting his friend have his moment.

'So it was him all along,' Adam said, finally. 'And the prick has thrown the painting away. What are we going to tell Maggie?' Adam asked.

Colin simply shook his head.

THE REST OF the day was spent in a cycle, with Colin relaying what he'd seen inside the room, and then extended periods of silence.

As well as Tex's body in the bath, there was the hand-written note and an iPad on the bed, left open on a webpage about an art auction on the day they arrived in Venice.

Adam's assumption had been that the guilt of planning to sell the painting at said auction is what had tipped Tex over the edge. The fact the webpage was open as he'd done the deed surely lent credence to that idea.

But, something wasn't sitting right with Colin.

It all felt too... set-up?

That wasn't quite the right sentiment to sum it up, but Colin was finding words hard to come by. In his mind, the open door to the bedroom, the note and the perfectly positioned iPad was all just a bit too convenient.

Though, they had been going there to accuse him of stealing the painting and there were no signs of a struggle, so who was to know?

The police would soon establish if it was a crime scene or not, though the inclusion of the note would surely lead them down a very opportune path. The guy was a suspected thief and the death had happened in international waters. He couldn't imagine the Venetian police force tripping over themselves to open up an investigation.

He also imagined that Captain Edd would push for that, too. A felo-de-se on his boat was bad enough, but even fouler play was worse. The phrase 'there's no such thing as bad publicity' didn't quite work here, and he imagined the cruise company owners would quite like the story of the dead art dealer to vanish as quickly as possible, and who could blame them?

Day turned to night, and slept crept up on Colin, who called it a night with his thoughts on the scrawled note.

14

REASONABLE DOUBT

SLEEP, THOUGH, HADN'T managed to keep a firm hold on Colin.

Every time he'd drifted off, images of Maggie floated into his mind. Maggie lying on the floor. Maggie's tears as she realised her beloved painting had been stolen. Future Maggie disembarking the ship, facing a life without her priceless heirloom.

It broke his heart, and short of dredging the ocean, he wasn't sure what he could do. And so, he'd spent most of the night staring at the ceiling, hoping inspiration would strike.

He kept thinking back, too, to Tex and the guilt that had driven him to take his own life. It was a horrible thing to say, but Colin was finding it hard to feel any sympathy for him. He'd stolen from an old lady, he'd lied about his involvement to Adam and him, and all for what? A quick buck, as the Americans would say.

Colin wondered if the art gallery in Venice would be annoyed that he'd gotten their hopes up by telling them that he was in possession of... whatever the painting was called. Colin couldn't quite remember, but knew it was similar to that character from Mean Girls, like Isiah had pointed out on the first night. Gretchen, was it?

And then something hit Colin like a lightning bolt. He grabbed his phone from the floor and pulled up the pictures, swiping until he got to the photo of the note Tex had left behind.

He skimmed the photo until he found the vital piece of information that blew this whole case wide open again. Without even looking at the time, he hollered Adam's name.

THE SHIP WAS sinking. Adam was sure of it. There couldn't be any other reason for such a volatile awakening.

Within a few seconds of hearing his name, he was bolt upright, his dressing gown already tightly wrapped around his body as he fled for the door.

His senses returned in incremental stages upon entering the suite's living space. Colin sat on the sofa, curled up under a duvet staring at his phone. That meant that the ship couldn't be in an emergency situation, and Adam's temper started to bubble.

'Did you call me?' Adam asked, his voice thick with sleep.

'Obviously, yeah,' Colin said. 'Who else is going to be shouting for you?'

'Do you know what bloody time it is?'

'No. Do you?'

'No, but I know it's early. Too early.' He rubbed his eyes. 'What's the matter?'

'Tex was killed.'

'Shut up.'

'I'm serious,' Colin said, tapping the sofa for Adam to sit down beside him. Obediently, Adam shuffled across and took his place, as requested.

'I can tell you now, this is going to be a hard sell,' Adam said.

'Allow me to make a believer from a disbeliever, Doubting Thomas.'

'Thomas?'

'The Disciple. Goodness me, your general knowledge is appalling.'

'I didn't get out of bed to be insulted,' Adam tutted. 'Tell me what you've found.'

'Right,' Colin began. 'Well, I know he was our main suspect for a while, but now it strikes me as odd that Tex would steal it in the first place. I mean, he's a fan of art, and he must come into contact with world famous pieces all the time.'

'Yeah, in galleries,' Adam said. 'Not just sitting at a dinner table with a dotty old woman and no security.'

'Fine, I take your point. But, don't call Maggie dotty again. If you do, I'll slap you.'

'Apologies.'

'Accepted,' Colin nodded. 'Now, even if Tex *had* stolen the painting, why would he throw it overboard. It doesn't make sense. You could tell he was absolutely blown away by seeing it in real life. Why would an art lover deprive the world of a true masterpiece?'

'Guilt?'

'Nah, I'm not buying that.'

'Your argument so far is what the police would call circumstantial, at best,' Adam said. 'Consider me unconvinced.'

'Okay,' Colin allowed. 'Allow me to present the coup de grâce.'

He passed Adam his phone and showed him the Google page for the stolen painting.

'Remember the name.'

'Grachten,' Adam mouthed.

'And now look at Tex's note.'

Adam navigated to the photos and pulled up the note.

'Cracthen' Adam said, puzzled.

'You're telling me that an art dealer is going to get the name of a famous painting wrong?'

'Jesus,' Adam said, stunned. 'So, what does this mean?'

'It means,' said Colin. 'That someone on this ship killed Tex and tried to pass it off as suicide by guilty conscience. And I think I know who.'

THEY MARCHED ALONG the deck, Colin on a mission and Adam urging him to see reason.

After finally being convinced of Tex's innocence, Colin had proceeded to tell Adam his theory.

Colin was convinced that Vaughn McClusky was behind the stolen painting and Tex's untimely demise. Adam had laughed at first, and when he saw that Colin was deadly serious, began to list the reasons why it couldn't be him.

1. He was rich enough to buy the painting if he wanted

2. He got paid double the painting's valuation on his last film alone

3. He was in the public eye. He was never going to put his career at risk for the sake of a quick buck

4. He'd been with them when Tex's body had been discovered

'Don't you think it's a coincidence that he started helping us, that he came with us to Tex's room, just as we discovered his body?' Colin asked.

'He *was* helping us. Helping being the key word here. Did you see his reaction when the body was found? He was white as a sheet. He ran off to get help.'

'He's an actor!' Colin said. 'Of course he's going to know how to react.'

'Dude, you're wrong on this one. Trust me.'

'Nope. I'm going to see him.'

'Then you're on your own.'

Adam stopped trying to talk sense into Colin and doubled back, hoping for a few more hours sleep. He felt bad arguing with his best friend, but he was starting to stress about the wedding, and was running low on energy and patience. What should have been a lovely, relaxing pre-wedding holiday had been the exact opposite, and he was very close to giving up.

Colin was wrong, and he could find that out alone.

COLIN WAS CONVINCED that the painting would be waiting behind Vaughn's door, and that taking the actor by surprise would be the best way of finding it.

He marched up to the door and knocked on it sharply three times, then pulled to the side so that he could not be seen through the spyhole. He could hear movement inside the room, but the door remained unopened.

After a minute, Colin knocked again, and a half-dressed Vaughn finally answered. Colin couldn't help but admire his chiselled abs and those cheekbones, though cursed himself for it.

'Colin, how are you? You feeling okay after yesterday?' he asked, stifling a yawn.

'Uh-huh,' Colin said. 'I was wondering if I could come in for a quick chat.'

'How about you give me a couple of minutes to get dressed,' Vaughn said, motioning to his pyjama bottoms and bare chest, 'and then I'll treat you to some breakfast?'

'Nah, it's cool,' Colin said, who took a step forward. 'It won't take long.'

'Seriously, mate, if you want to chat, let's chat, but not here, just give me…' Vaughn turned to look behind him, and Colin seized his chance. He ducked under the actor's arm and took a few steps into the room.

'What the bloody hell do you think you're doing?' Vaughn thundered.

'I think you're hiding something,' Colin said. 'I think you have the painting.'

'The painting is at the bottom of the ocean.'

'That's what the phoney suicide note said,' Colin answered.

'Phoney?'

'Yeah, phoney. As in someone else wrote it for Tex after he was killed.'

'Killed?' Vaughn repeated. 'Nonsense. Look, it's a traumatic thing seeing a body…'

'I've seen plenty,' Colin interrupted. 'Now, if you don't have it, you won't mind me looking around.'

'I don't have it, but I absolutely do mind you looking around. It's my bloody suite.'

Colin took a look around the room from where he stood, though there was no sign of the painting. He glanced sideways at the bedroom door, took a step towards it, when Vaughn growled.

'Don't you dare.'

As quick as a flash, Colin darted towards the door, and heard Vaughn's footsteps behind him. He made it through the door before Vaughn tackled him heavily to the floor.

'I told you not to…' Vaughn said, raising his fist.

Colin was spared a punch thanks to a well-timed intervention from the bed. A beautiful woman, wearing very little, pleaded with the actor not to get violent.

Vaughn nodded, and let his arm fall to his side, before letting Colin to his feet.

'Colin, meet Samantha.'

The woman covered herself with the duvet, and extended a hand in Colin's direction, which he shook.

'The reason I didn't want you barging in here is that Sam works on the ship, and employee-guest relations are strictly prohibited. We wouldn't want my companion here getting into any trouble now, would we?' Vaughn said.

'Sorry,' Colin said, sheepishly. 'I didn't mean to intrude.'

'Well, intrude you did. Can you keep this under your hat?'

'I don't care who you are sleeping with. I only care about the painting.'

'I appreciate that. I want poor Maggie to get the painting back as much as you do. Tell me about the faked note.'

'Nah, don't worry about it. I'm probably reading too much into it. I'll let you get back to… it.'

Colin bolted out of the bedroom and out of the front door, grateful for the fresh sea air that filled his lungs and cooled his cheeks, which were burning like a furnace. He felt like he was losing his marbles.

He had convinced himself that Vaughn was behind it all, when really, like Adam said, he *had* only been helpful the entire time. In desperation, Colin was simply lashing out at anyone he could think of.

He resolved to make things right with Vaughn before they reached Italy. He thought about going back to see him now, but decided to let him cool off for a while. He didn't fancy being on the receiving end of a fist, should Vaughn change his mind. As he started to walk towards his own cabin, he thought he caught sight of someone peering at him from around the corner.

When he looked again, they were gone. Colin ran to the end of the passageway, and hurtled around the corner.

There was no one there. The corridor was completely empty.

He stood for a while, in the hope that whoever had been there (if they had been at all) would be forced out of their hiding place. After a few minutes, and no movement, Colin gave up.

Perhaps it had been a trick of the light, he thought, as he turned and made his way back to his own cabin.

WITH HIS TAIL tucked firmly between his legs, Colin grovelled apologies to Adam, who accepted graciously, even after Colin had told him about stumbling into Vaughn's bedroom to find a mostly-nude woman in his bed.

'I doubt he's going to be buying us any more whisky,' Adam laughed. 'But, who cares? We're getting off the boat tomorrow, and not a moment too soon.'

'Should we get drunk and forget about the painting?' Colin asked.

In reply, Adam opened the door to their cabin and ushered Colin out of it.

They chose a bar as far away from first class as they could, and set about draining the place of every drop of alcohol available.

The evening quickly became a blur, and involved karaoke. Adam brought out his version of Livin' On A Prayer, though struggled to hit the high notes and messed up the key change. He was applauded for his efforts by the friendly crowd who had gathered, though Colin did note some people with their fingers plugging their ears long after he'd left the stage.

Colin refused to bow to peer pressure and resisted the stage, instead ordering another round of drinks.

Mid-way through that drink, Adam's phone rang and he held up the screen to show that it was Helena.

'Probably time to be going, anyway,' Colin said. 'You head on and chat to your good lady, and I'll finish my drink.'

Adam gave him a slobbery kiss on the cheek and left the bar, professing his love to Helena as soon as he'd answered the call.

Colin sat back and savoured his pint. The woman on stage was storming through a version of 'Waterloo', much to the delight of a middle-aged couple who had taken residence on the dancefloor. When he was done with his drink, he got up from his seat and left the bar.

The ship was skirting the Italian coast now, the twinkling lights of the cities a welcome sign to Colin. He would be glad to set foot on land again, see Anna, and hopefully forget the whole debacle, though the shame of not being able to get Maggie's painting back would surely haunt him.

He made it to his room, and stood by the balcony outside, appreciating the view. He heard the footsteps too late.

Before he could react, someone had kicked his knees and he'd toppled to the floor. Punches and kicks rained down on him, and, somewhat ridiculously, Colin's only thought was to protect his face for the wedding photographs. He crawled into the foetal position and curled his arms around his head, as a pair of boots and knobbly knuckles took aim at his ribs and legs.

Despite the beating, Colin's main thoughts were on the strangely out of place sound. It sounded like whoever was attacking him was shaking a maraca. A quiet chk-chk-chk noise punctuated the spaces between Colin's grunts and shouts.

As soon as it had started, it was over, thanks to an approaching drunken couple. Colin breathed a sigh of relief, and lay listening as the offending footsteps retreated, and the couple rushed to his aid.

15

GOTCHA

'IT'S A GOOD thing,' Colin said, over breakfast, which they'd ordered to their room.

'A good thing? Are you off your head?' Adam spat.

'It means there is someone on the ship who wants us out of the way.'

'Ah, you're right! That *is* a good thing,' Adam said, sarcastically.

'Don't be hysterical,' Colin said, wincing in pain as he adjusted his position on the sofa.

'Me? Hysterical? Why would I be hysterical? I mean, I'm getting married in two days and my best man, my best friend in the world, has just taken a kicking from an unknown assailant.'

'Look,' Colin said. 'It means that whoever took the painting obviously doesn't like us looking into it, especially as Venice draws nearer. They thought they were home and dry, that we'd give up after their failed Tex set-up. Not only are they a thief, they're a murderer, too.'

'It has to be Vaughn!' Adam said, jumping up.

'What do you mean?'

'You went to see him, barged into his room and then took a beating. He's the only person we've spoken to since you realised the whole Tex thing was a red herring.'

'He's the only person we've spoken to, but I forgot to tell you about something. When I left his room, I was sure I saw someone watching me. When I ran towards them, they were gone.'

'What? They disappeared into thin air?' Adam looked sceptical.

'It made me think that there wasn't really anyone there at the time, but maybe whoever it was saw that we were still investigating and tried to take me out.'

'That would leave Henry and Sean.'

'Hazza,' Colin corrected.

'Nah, Hazza is what his friends call him, and we are no friends of his.'

The rest of the morning was spent plotting. Venice was only a few hours away, and they wanted to speak to each of their suspects. They reasoned that whoever attacked Colin last night would not feel as confident in handing out a beating in the daylight hours, or with so many people around, so it was safe to split up to cover both bases.

Colin would try and find Sean, and Adam would track down Hazza.

COLIN WINCED WITH each step, pain flaring in every joint and nerve, or so it seemed.

For once, the size of the ship was against him, and he spent an unhappy half hour toddling around, unable to summon up the reserves of strength to make much of a go of it.

Frustrated, he stopped at a coffee shop and found a table in the back corner, where he sat clutching a bottle of water with his head down on the cool surface of the table, hoping Adam wouldn't come this way and see him at such a low ebb.

He'd put on a decent show for Adam earlier, trying to play down the incident, but the truth was he was scared. It was unbelievable that there was someone on the boat who would attack, steal and kill, and that they were still roaming free.

With that awful idea in his head, he took a deep breath, steadied himself and then carefully hoisted himself up from his seat. He hoped and prayed that if he did come across Sean, that he didn't have to put up too much of a fight.

ON THE OTHER side of the ship, Adam was hunting for Hazza like a man possessed.

Sweat pooled on his back and in his armpits, such was the ferocity of his search, but he didn't let that bother him. Instead, he picked up the pace.

He poked his head into every bar, café and shop he came to. He barged into the spa and scared the receptionist half to death with the ferocity with which he barked Hazza's name. The poor woman shook her head and ran into the back room.

Adam felt bad, but only momentarily. He was sure the spa's guarantee to relax and rejuvenate worked on the employees, too. She'd be kicking back, stress-free in no time.

Unlike him.

He could feel the muscles in his shoulders tighten, as they often did when he was feeling stressed out.

After another fruitless half-an-hour, he was ready to give up, when he realised he'd not checked the most obvious place. They'd stumbled across Hazza in the casino when they went looking the first time (which felt like months ago). Perhaps he was there again?

Adam travelled up an escalator and made his way down the corridor, where the sounds of jubilation and despair began to fill the air. He turned into the casino, where gamblers were hunched slot machines, cashing in chips and refilling drinks at the well-stocked bar.

He studied each table, spotting Hazza at the far side of the room, staring intently at the playing cards in his left hand. After ten seconds, he set his cards down and pushed some more coloured chips into the middle.

Adam stood for a while, watching him, wondering if he was their man. Eventually, he decided there was nothing to be found out from being on the other side of the room, so started to make his way over.

And then he saw it.

He realised that while he'd been watching, Hazza had been using his left hand for everything. Checking his cards. Pushing the chips. Pouring the fruity cocktail into his mouth.

Now, he raised his right hand to scratch his nose, and Adam was surprised to see that it was bandaged. Hazza grimaced like the action was causing him pain, and Adam knew why.

Hazza was the one who had beat up Colin.

In a flash of rage, Adam marched across the floor, picking up speed as he went. When he neared his target, he was almost running. All the stress of the past few weeks seemed to melt away as he rugby tackled Hazza onto the card table, causing chips to scatter like broken glass, and a series of audible gasps arose from those who had been enjoying their game just seconds before.

'Get the captain,' Adam shouted to the dealer. 'This man is trouble.'

16

THE ROGUE

EDD HAD TAKEN the accusations against Hazza extremely seriously, and had come to the casino to find Hazza struggling under Adam's weight, who in turn was straddling him in an imitation of a citizen's arrest he'd seen Mark perform on *Peep Show* once.

Hazza continued to protest his innocence, but complied with the captain's orders to go with him until the police arrived. Adam had passed Edd his mobile number, as he was keen to hear what decision the Venetian police came to.

He returned to the cabin to find Colin slumped on the sofa, and relayed what had just happened.

'You tackled him onto the table?' Colin repeated.

'Yeah. Maybe I went a bit far, but when I saw that bandage, I thought of him beating you up, and I lost it.'

'I'd hug you if I could,' Colin said. 'But I think it might hurt my ribs.'

The ship was slowing now, on its final approach into Venice. The boys watched from the balcony, and were blown away by the beauty of the place. Their train north to Lake Garda wasn't until later that evening, and Adam was looking forward to spending a few care-free hours wandering the streets of Italy's watery wonderland.

They had packed earlier that morning, though having mostly lived out of a suitcase, it hadn't taken long. Now, they scooped up the last items and shoved them in their cases, before checking under the bed and in nooks and crannies for odd socks and the likes.

Then, they said goodbye to their room and made their way towards the first floor for the final disembarkation, with one detour en route.

When Maggie opened her door, she was dressed in a flowing, colourful dress.

'We thought we'd come and say bye,' Colin said. 'We're so sorry we couldn't be more help.'

She pulled him into a tight hug, and told him to stop being silly. It was time to forget about the painting, she said, and move on.

Adam filled her in with the latest developments, and she smiled. A little bit of hope twinkled in her eye. She held up a finger, and disappeared into her room, reappearing a few minutes later with an envelope, which she handed to Adam.

He tried to resist, though she insisted.

'Treat yourself and your good lady wife to a wee treat on honeymoon,' she said, and gave him a hug too.

They said their goodbyes, and Adam and Colin made their way to the exit.

Looking around, Adam was sad that they hadn't utilised the ship to its full potential. There were so many parts of The Elysian that they hadn't even been to, so focused were they on trying to retrieve the painting.

Still, it had been for a noble cause, and hopefully the police would be able to interrogate Hazza and find out where he'd hidden the painting.

A huge crowd had gathered in the vast expanse of space, eager to get off and explore a new city. There was a buzz in the air; an infectious one. It was time to forget about what had happened over the past week, and focus on what was to come.

The wedding!

His thoughts of "I Dos" by the lakeside were shattered by a commotion on the other side of the waiting area. There was some jostling, and Adam assumed it was the normal bustle that came with being part of a crowd, and went back to his daydream. Then, he saw a flash of unruly ginger hair.

It was Sean, shoving his way through the assembled passengers, trying to get as close to the door as possible. Adam watched as his rucksack collided with a little girl's head. Her father shouted after Sean, but he was almost at the door, which had just opened.

'Someone's in a hurry,' Colin said, having also noticed the hubbub.

'I wonder did he make any inroads with a new job,' Adam replied.

'Who knows?' Colin said. 'I'm looking forward to never thinking about any of these people again. Especially Vaughn, who I never got the chance to apologise to. Hopefully we don't see him before we leave!'

The crowd was pouring through the door now, making their way towards the city.

Colin and Adam's plan was simple. Walk to the nearby train station, stow their cases in a locker so that they didn't have to cart them around all day, and then enjoy their day. Adam couldn't wait to visit Ciao Gelato. He'd researched the best ice-cream shop in Venice long before they'd arrived, and discovered they did a honeycomb and white chocolate mix. He was eager to get moving!

The train station wasn't far, but it took longer than anticipated, on account of Colin's bruised and battered body. When they arrived, they stuffed their cases in a yellow locker, deposited a couple of Euros in the slot and collected the key.

Just then, Adam's phone rang. It was a number he didn't recognise.

'Hello.'

'Is this Adam?'

'Yes.'

'It's Edd, here. I just wanted to let you know that Henry's story checked out. He claimed he cut his hand helping a barmaid pick up a smashed glass. We spoke to the barmaid in question and she confirmed the story. The police have also searched his room and didn't find the painting. They are letting him go, though they are going to investigate Mr Rivera's death. You might need to give a statement, as you were there when the body was discovered, though they might be happy with my version of events. Am I okay to pass your number on?'

'Yeah, no problem,' Adam said. 'Thanks for letting me know.'

Adam communicated the content of the phone call to Colin, who closed his eyes and sighed.

'It's Sean, isn't it?' he said

'That might explain why he looked so eager to get off the boat this morning,' Adam nodded.

'At least we know where he'll be.'

Colin pulled out his phone and swiped through the photos. He stopped on the picture of the iPad on Tex's bed, that was open on a website of an art auction due to take place today in Venice, today. Colin mouthed the address a few times, and then typed it into Google Maps. The little blue line showed them that the auction house wasn't too far away.

'I say we go catch our thief red-handed!' Adam said.

ESPOSITO'S AUCTIONEERS WAS housed in a stunning little building. Near the Bridge of Sighs, it was tucked away in a little back street. The stonework may have been ageing, but it was doing so gracefully. Ivy crept across the façade, trimmed away near the narrow windows, and a small, gold sign beside the door was in keeping with the tasteful décor. A well-dressed man welcomed them in Italian, handing them a brochure which they accepted.

Inside was a flurry of activity.

At the front of the room, an auctioneer with an ornate wooden gavel in his hand was speaking at the speed of light, motioning to a canvas on an easel next to him and trying (Adam assumed) to enthuse the bidders into upping the price. At the side, a row of smartly dressed employees had phones to their ears and fingers whirling over computer keyboards, presumably communicating with would-be bidders who couldn't make it to the Venetian auction house.

There were three auction-goers locked in a bidding war, one raising his numbered paddle covertly, the others not bothering to mask their passion for the prize on offer.

Eventually, paddle man backed out, leaving a two-horse race.

The man with the round glasses and clean-shaven face was not to be outdone, and finally triumphed. He looked delighted at the win, and shook hands with his adversary, who congratulated him passionately.

Adam was wondering if an auction in the UK would end so cordially, when he spotted a tense looking Sean on the far side of the room, twirling a strand of his long, ginger hair around one of his fingers, and staring at the auctioneer like the man might give him the secrets to everlasting life.

Adam and Colin didn't want to make a scene, so they took a seat and bided their time. Adam concluded that it would have been an enjoyable way to spend an hour, except for the fact they were about to try and apprehend a killer.

On the penultimate lot, Sean suddenly became animated. The painting was quite bleak; a row of houses separated by a glowing river of fire. There were three suns in the sky, though they provided no light for the land. Adam found the whole scene very unsettling.

Sean, though, seemed to like it very much as he was using his paddle to great effect. There was only one other person in the room who seemed to be interested, and even they dropped out reasonably quickly.

Following a fist pump, Sean got to his feet and walked to the payment desk. Colin kept an eye on him while the final painting was wheeled out. They had both assumed that the famous stolen painting would be kept until last, perhaps as a surprise, as it wasn't listed in the auction catalogue.

When it was unveiled, they were dismayed to see that it was not Maggie's painting.

'Maybe it sold before we got here?' Adam suggested.

'Maybe,' Colin shrugged. 'But why would he hang about? Surely if you'd stolen a painting and sold it illegally for millions, you'd want to get out as soon as possible.'

'Agreed. Maybe he's waiting for the payment to go through?'

They watched Sean finish at the finance desk, shake hands with the employee who had dealt with him, and make his way towards the door. Adam and Colin followed him outside, into the small courtyard at the front of the building, where they called his name.

Sean spun on the spot; confusion plastered across his face.

'Lads, ye alright?'

'Grand,' Colin nodded. 'You must be buzzing.'

'I am, aye. What are you doing here?'

'Well, we thought Hazza was behind the painting theft. As a matter of fact, we left him for the police to deal with on the ship, but it seems his story checked out, and they've let him go. And then, we see you hotfooting it off the ship and, lo and behold, you end up at the very auction Tex had been planning to attend. Bit odd, no?'

'Not really, pal. I had nothing to do with the old lady's painting, like I already told you.'

'Why are you buzzing then?' Adam asked.

'Because Tex gave me a tip off about an up-and-coming artist who he believed is going to make it big. One of his pieces was going up for sale today, and Tex had told me he reckoned it was a good investment opportunity, so I was eager to get here. And, I won it at well below what he thought it was worth.'

'But...' Adam started.

'Look, lads, short of putting my hand on my heart and swearing I wasn't involved, I don't know what I have to do to convince you.' He turned to go, and then spoke again. 'Oh, by the way, what did you do to the actor?'

'Vaughn?' Colin said. 'Why?'

'Well, I was near his room when I saw you come out of it, but I hid round the corner.'

'Why?'

'Because I couldn't be arsed with the hassle of talking to you. All you've done the whole holiday is ask questions and throw accusations around, and I didn't have time for that. Anyway, not long after you'd left, I crept out of my hiding place and Vaughn was outside his room, downing some of those pills he always carried around with him. He looked furious. He saw me and asked had I seen you, but I lied and said no. He looked like he wanted to kill you.'

Adam and Colin shared a look.

'Well, anyway boys,' Sean said. 'I'd be lying if I said it was good to see you again. See ye!'

And with that he sauntered out of the courtyard, and out of their lives.

17

ALAN SUGAR WOULD BE TERRIFIED
OF THIS BOARDROOM

VAUGHN MCCLUSKY PULLED out a little handheld mirror from his pocket and checked himself out.

Though a crack ran the length of the glass, it didn't stop him admiring how suave he looked, even if he did say so himself. The suit he'd just bought at the most exclusive tailor in the city hugged his muscular figure; the facial and haircut he'd had that afternoon had got him right in the mood for business.

He was ready to close this deal; the one that would take his career into the next level.

A little flutter of nervousness reminded him that a meeting with Mr Palmer was not something to be trifled with. The man was shrewd, and needed to know that there was serious investment and intent behind a project before he'd even consider putting his name to it.

Hell, owning a yacht that was moored in Venice was not something that happened by being a pushover, and Mr Palmer was certainly no pushover.

Still, Vaughn liked to think that his little gift would sweeten the deal before they even got to talking about the numbers. He was confident that come the end of the night (or the next morning, depending on how the party panned out), he'd be leaving the yacht with what he needed.

That nervousness was still there, though, so he shouted through the partition of the limo, telling the driver to take care while he made a drink. He felt the car slow by a few miles per hour, and reached towards the well-stocked drinks tray, grabbing the bottle of his favourite brandy and a lowball tumbler. He added a few ice cubes, and swirled the contents, his eyes drifting to the window and the passing Venetians who had no idea a genuine movie star was in their midst.

Ten minutes, and another drink, later, the limo pulled to a smooth stop in one of the private parking spaces reserved for guests Mr Palmer's. The driver, a little man with a bulging belly wearing an ill-fitting suit, opened the door for Vaughn, who got out and waited while the chauffeur pulled his bags out of the boot.

Vaughn tipped him and made his way towards the superyacht. It really was a thing of beauty, all sleek lines and sophisticated details. Even the gangplank, which he took his time on, looked like it had been sculpted by a master of his craft.

He was greeted at the top of the steps by Mr Palmer's personal assistant, Doris Braine, who always seemed immune to his flirtatious charms. He often thought that maybe it was part of her job description. After all, not many women of the world could remain resistant to his magnetism once he really turned it on. Doris had remained a tough nut to crack, but he wasn't one to shy away from a challenge.

She led him through a series of passageways, past walnut doors and gleaming white walls, into the bowels of the ship. They were underwater now; he could hear the water slapping against the side of the yacht.

'Is Mr Palmer in a good mood?' Vaughn asked.

'When is he not?' Doris said, without looking back.

Vaughn shook his head at her aloofness.

They turned one last corner and there in front of them, behind a door of frosted glass, was the fabled board room. Vaughn could only imagine the deals that had been struck in this room. Palmer had produced some of the greatest films of this century, and Vaughn felt his palms grow slightly damp at the prospect of being part of his canon.

Doris held the door open, and Vaughn brushed past, slightly closer than was necessary, but what was a bit of harmless fun between friends?

'Who do I have to hump around here to get a scotch on the rocks?' he said to her, before striding towards one of the comfy chairs dotted around the huge oak slab of a table.

His mind was still on Doris's rump when he sat down, so much so that it was only as he looked up that he noticed Adam and Colin sitting across the boardroom table from him, next to Mr Palmer.

'What the...' he started.

COLIN WATCHED HIM harass the PA and stride into the room like he owned the place, and wondered why he hadn't seen that Vaughn was behind all of this sooner. He'd had a hunch, which he'd followed, but the film star's charisma, as well as Adam's doubts, had thrown him off the scent.

It was almost funny to watch the instantaneous change in Vaughn's demeanour, from king of the world to dumbstruck pauper. It was even funnier when his eyes settled on Grachten, which was hanging on the wall above Mr Palmer's head.

'I imagine you'd like to know why we're gate crashing your million-pound meeting,' Adam said, once Vaughn had sat down.

Vaughn opened and closed his mouth like a beached guppy, his eyes flitting between Adam, Colin and Mr Palmer, who was watching him with not an iota of expression on his face.

'Cat got your tongue?' Adam continued. 'No worries. We've got you bang to rights anyway, so you can sit back, shut up, and enjoy our little presentation. Colin?'

'Thank you, Adam,' Colin said. 'I'd like to start by saying you fight like a bitch. I mean, what type of man attacks someone from behind?'

'The kind of man who would steal from an old lady,' Adam interjected. 'An absolute scumbag.'

'Ah, yes. You see, Vaughn, we finally got there. Might have taken us a little longer than usual, but you were a worthy adversary. Shall I talk you through our little journey of discovery?'

Vaughn simply stared, so Colin went on.

'Firstly, your little box of pills. You didn't mind flaunting them while regaling everyone with your little backstory. Good for sympathy, that well-known battle with illness that ended with you losing an organ. No spleen means a poor immune system, which means a couple of phenoxymethalpennicillin every day to keep you right. Although, that's not all you're taking, is it? We did a bit of research, found out about your sleeping pill addiction. That little box you carry with you rattles like a musical instrument, what with you taking four pills each day, and when you were kicking and punching me while I was on the floor, I thought I heard a maraca. I thought I was losing my mind at the time, but that's what made me finally realise it was you.'

He left out the fact that he'd needed a further clue from Sean to put the two facts together.

'The second clue was Poor Tex's bedroom,' Adam took over. 'The room looked too set up, so we figured it must've been staged. Granted, we only came to that conclusion in the past hour or so, but who better to stage someone taking their own life than someone who spends their own life on a set? I imagine when they open Tex up, they'll find some of your sleeping pills in his blood. It didn't look like he put up too much of a fight.'

'And the third, and possibly the most irrefutable fact, is that you sent the painting from Lisbon to Mr Palmer, here, via courier. You could've chosen any name in the world as an alias, but you had to choose Len Fist, the name of your character in Jawbone. The arrogance is mind-blowing.'

Colin laughed out loud, which seemed to stir Vaughn into action. He jumped up from his chair, and started to march towards the door.

'Sit yourself down,' Mr Palmer said, producing a gun from a holster that had been hidden below his jacket.

Vaughn stopped in his tracks. He turned to face the table again. 'You're not going to shoot me.'

'Try me,' Palmer replied. The calmness in his voice was unnerving.

Vaughn hesitated, and looked like he was about to call Palmer's bluff, just as the board room door flew open and several Venetian police officers barrelled through at the same time, knocking Vaughn to the ground where they wrenched his arms behind his back and tightened handcuffs around his wrists. He tried to put up a fight, but a few sly kicks to the ribs did the trick of quietening him.

Unbelievably, as he was led out of the yacht by the unimpressed Venetian police, he was screaming about how much the suit cost.

'How long until our train?' Colin asked.

'Enough time to reunite Grachten and Maggie,' Adam said.

Mr Palmer rose from his seat, took the painting off the hook on the wall and passed it to Colin. Before coming to his yacht, they'd worried that he wouldn't believe them, or insist on keeping the painting, but he'd been very keen to see justice done. It had been his idea to lure Vaughn into the boardroom for the showdown.

'You could make a movie from Vaughn's little escapade,' Colin joked as Palmer waved them off the yacht.

'You know what?' he said. 'I just might.'

18

I DO, I DO, I DO, I DO, I DO

IT WAS A perfect day for a perfect wedding. The sun was shining, and a light breeze ruffled Adam's hair. His nearest and dearest were assembled on one of the elevated terraces of the medieval Scaligero Castle, with views overlooking the endless lake and jagged mountains. It was picture perfect.

He and Colin had already been here for a few hours, sorting the chairs, blowing up balloons, and helping the old caretaker erect the cream canopy, under which Adam and Helena would be saying their vows.

He'd had a couple of wobbles. It was all feeling very real now, and he started to panic about forgetting the vows, or falling over, or farting loudly during a key part of the ceremony. He'd already asked Colin if he had the rings three times.

Once the guests had started to arrive, Adam had relaxed a bit, safe in the knowledge that everyone in attendance was rooting for them, though he had shed a few tears as he'd greeted his mum.

Now, Adam's heart started to beat overtime as the string quartet plucked the first notes of Canon In D, signalling Helena's arrival at the end of the aisle. He heard gasps from the congregation as she made her way towards him, and only turned to look at her when she was by his side.

Adam spent a few moments taking her in. The stunning ivory dress (that fitted perfectly, thank God), the subtle make-up that accentuated those spectacular eyes, the delicate kink in her dark hair.

'You look beautiful,' he whispered. 'I love your dress.'

'Thanks,' she replied. 'It has pockets.'

She hammered home the point by shoving her hands in them, which Adam nodded at.

'You don't look so bad yourself,' she smiled.

With that, the vicar began the ceremony, which passed in a blur of song and repeated vows and applause. When it was time to kiss the bride, Adam caught his mum's eye, grimaced, mouthed an apology to her and gave Helena a peck on the lips.

They walked hand in hand down the aisle as a married couple to "You Make My Dreams" by Hall and Oates, receiving pats on the back and hugs, while multicoloured confetti was thrown over them. Helena shot a confused look at an old woman in a snazzy dress who was sitting at the end of one of the rows, clutching a framed painting.

ON THE SECLUDED beach, accessible by a secret door in the bowels of the old castle, they finally had a moment to themselves.

Well, almost.

A very passionate Italian photographer was directing them, making them hug and kiss and cuddle against the magnificent backdrop of the lake. He'd make them repeat a pose, or hold it for a ridiculous amount of time until the light was just right, or a wave crested at just the right time behind them.

Adam was finding the whole thing very awkward, and was sure he looked like some sort of uncomfortable stick insect in most of the snaps the photographer had taken so far.

Next, he made them attempt to skim some of the shale that littered the beach on the glassy surface of the lake.

'I wish he'd hurry up and finish,' Adam whispered to Helena, as he tossed a stone towards the water. The sunlight reflected off his ring, and he rotated it on his finger, wondering how long it would take it feel normal.

'I know. It's a bit of a nightmare,' Helena replied. 'Oh, I never got a chance to ask. How was the cruise in the end?'

'Aye, it was good,' Adam nodded.

'And you managed to stay out of trouble?' she asked.

'Mostly, yeah,' he said. 'Colin didn't manage to stop me having a go at the karaoke.'

She laughed, and Adam heard the click of the photographer's camera. At least there'll be one natural looking photo, he thought.

Adam had deliberated on how much to tell his new bride, and reckoned honesty was the best policy, especially on his wedding day. Best to start the rest of their lives with no secrets between them.

'Oh, and you know Vaughn McClusky?'

'The movie star you like?' she said.

'Yeah. Well, we managed to get him arrested for stealing a painting from an old lady, so he's going to be going to jail.'

'What?!' she gasped.

As if God was smiling down on him, the photographer decided he had what he needed from this particular scene, and proceeded to tell them what he wanted them to do next.

Adam was suddenly very interested in what he had to say.

AUTHOR'S NOTE

Here we are, at the end of book six!

When Sean at Red Dog Press offered me a six book deal for the Stonebridge series, I snapped his hand off, thinking myself very lucky. I have loved writing each book, and it has been absolutely humbling to have found a readership that cares for the characters as much as I do.

Adam and Colin have changed so much over the course of the series. Listening to The Curious Dispatch of Daniel Costello made me realise how green behind the gills they were, purposefully so, and it's lovely to see them mature and find their place in the world.

I'm very lucky that, thanks to YOU, the series can continue, and the boys will still be a fixture in my life. This is down to you wonderful readers, who continue to support me with your kindness. With thousands of authors and millions of books on offer, it still blows me away that you are choosing to spend your hard-earned cash on words that I've written.

I'm also hugely thankful to Isis Audio and Stephen Armstrong for bringing this particular little corner of Northern Ireland to life through the audiobooks. I don't think I've ever felt as proud of anything in my life as when I listened to that opening chapter of Danny Costello.

I hope you continue to enjoy your trips to Stonebridge.

Love,

Chris

ABOUT THE AUTHOR

Originally hailing from the north coast of Northern Ireland and now residing in South Manchester, Chris McDonald has always been a reader. At primary school, The Hardy Boys inspired his love of adventure, before his reading world was opened up by Chuck Palahniuk and the gritty world of crime.

He's a fan of 5-a-side football, has an eclectic taste in music ranging from Damien Rice to Slayer and loves dogs.

Printed in Great Britain
by Amazon